PRAISE FOR M

"Sary's instinct for the miraculous is indeed strong in this tender novel that lovingly captures the yearning for human connection."

-Donia Bijan, author of *The Last Days of Cafe Leila*

"I was transfixed by this novel set in a town suffused with ghosts figurative and literal, and moved deeply to witness an eccentric woman's grief transmuted into a gripping testament to the power of the individual imagination."

-Antoine Wilson, author of *Mouth to Mouth*

"Beautifully written and satisfyingly creepy, this is one of the most poignant and original ghost stories I've ever read."

-Mark Haskell Smith, author of *Blown*

"*Magdalena* is a unique and beautiful story, one framed by a mystery that propels the reader swiftly through its pages. Sary's tale of love, loss and maternal devotion pulls hard at the heartstrings and is impossible to put down."

-Diane Haeger, best-selling author of *Courtesan*

"In a small seaside town haunted by ghosts and run by the Catholic church a woman finds unexpected power in telling her own story. A quirky and suspenseful read!"

-Katya Apekina, author of *The Deeper the Water the Uglier the Fish*

"Is it possible to write a modern day ghost story that's also a poignant tale about love, loss, and redemption? Candi Sary has done just that with her second novel, *Magdalena*. Shirley Jackson fans will be kicking up their heels."

-Barbara DeMarco-Barrett, author of *Palm Springs Noir* (Akashic) and host of Writers on Writing

"Ghostly and mysterious yet rooted in the claustrophobic reality of a small town, *Magdalena* investigates a woman's search for connection to the idiosyncratic people who cross her path, and most of all, to herself. This dark and delicate novel is a mesmeric read."

-Siel Ju, author of *Cake Time*

"*Magdalena* took me into a world of obsessive love and the desperation we all have for connection in this world and the next. Candi Sary lured me into the heart of Dottie, her misfit narrator whose loyalty carries her up and out of loneliness and tragedy. Once you get started, you won't put it down and you won't want it to end."

-Mary Castillo, author of The Dori O. Paranormal Mystery Series

"*Magdalena* is a ghost story about the living, in which the ghosts are less haunting than the lives of the characters themselves. Candi Sary tells an honest and heartfelt story about outcasts and the ghosts that haunt them, as they struggle to find their place in a small town rife with gossip. Executed with enchanting prose, the story unfolds with such a captivating sequence of events that it is hard to put down and even harder to forget."

-Amy R. Biddle, author of *The Atheist's Prayer* and co-founder of Underground Book Reviews

"Candi Sary's newest novel, *Magdalena*, follows her central character, Dottie, as she maneuvers through her small life, small town, and unfortunate circumstances. We watch as she seeks comfort in a young girl's presence, or is it obsession? Sary's mesmerizing writing style envelopes the reader in the dreamlike reality of Dottie's nontraditional ways of overcoming grief."

-Nancy Klann-Moren, author of *The Clock Of Life*

"This compelling novel tells the story of a hero's journey achieved by a woman. Candi Sary's astonishing fable locates us inside Dottie's mind as she traverses the ghostly underworld of Sam's Town and discovers her own power to rescue herself, teenage Magdalena, and the entire town."

-Stephanie Golden, author of *Slaying the Mermaid: Women and the Culture of Sacrifice*

"Sary draws us into a paranormal tale that feels absolutely real, heavy and creepily familiar. Layers of a mysterious past draw the reader into the narrator's world, a lonely woman who carries the weight of more than one ghost. Absolutely impactful, *Magdalena* is a clearly told, multi-layered drama that pulls us into a troubled town and a haunted life—even compelling the reader to confront their own phantoms."

-Dominic Carrillo, author of *Acts of Resistance*

MAGDALENA

Candi Sary

Regal House Publishing

Published by
Regal House Publishing, LLC
Raleigh, NC 27605
All rights reserved

ISBN -13 (paperback): 9781646033348
ISBN -13 (epub): 9781646033355
Library of Congress Control Number: 2022942692

Cover images and design by © C. B. Royal

Regal House Publishing, LLC
https://regalhousepublishing.com

The following is a work of fiction created by the author. All names, individuals, characters, places, items, brands, events, etc. were either the product of the author or were used fictitiously. Any name, place, event, person, brand, or item, current or past, is entirely coincidental.

Printed in the United States of America

For Tony, Rusty, and Cinnamon

You are my heart

"No live organism can continue for long to exist sanely under conditions of absolute reality: even larks and katydids are supposed, by some, to dream."
- Shirley Jackson

PROLOGUE

In my dream they're both still with me, the girl and the ghost. Their presence is so strong something inside of me, even in sleep, awakens. I watch from above and see myself on my living room couch, a slender woman with the kind of sloping shoulders that come with being too tall. Thin hair, pale skin, I'm not much to look at. There's a fifteen-year-old girl sitting beside me with long thick hair, warm brown skin, and the kind of confidence that comes with being born beautiful. Somewhere between us is the ghost only the girl can see and I distinctly feel. Nothing happens in my dream. The ghost doesn't move things around the house anymore. The girl doesn't busy herself with her phone anymore. We just sit together as if understanding it's only a dream, and maybe if we stay still enough, we can hold onto this miraculous time together again. While there appears to be no change in the scene for the entire length of the dream, by the end, I notice my shoulders have risen up. I'm sitting tall the way the girl sits. It's only a slight difference in my appearance but I'm struck by how unusual it looks on me. While the girl and I share few physical characteristics, our silhouettes now resemble each other. It's as if once someone has come into your life and made an imprint, it can change the very shape of you.

When I wake, I don't feel changed anymore. Not here in this sad room where they've put me. I prefer the lights out so I don't have to see what I've become. I just want to close my eyes and fall back to sleep and dream again about the girl and the ghost, and how we were before I lost them.

1

Magdalena once told me she knew how to cure sadness. She read on that little phone of hers that we all need fifteen minutes of sun every day and without it, depression could set in. Those of us here on the peninsula barely get fifteen minutes a week. The fog comes in over the cliffs in the morning, creeping through town, shrouding all neighborhoods with a thick graveyard effect. We don't have an actual graveyard, but the landslide all those years ago took enough lives and left enough ghosts behind to bring on that kind of fog. If it does lift around midmorning, a heavy cloud cover still stays most of the day, keeping things gray. I'd always thought my sadness came from the unfortunate things that happened in my life, but according to Magdalena, my gloom might simply be a lack of vitamin D.

From the day she got the phone, she stared into it constantly, seeking answers to all of her questions and even finding new questions she would have never thought of on her own. She fed on its information like meat.

"Mushrooms," Magdalena said. "We need to eat mushrooms." The girl was my only visitor. When she spoke, I hung on to her every word. "If we eat enough of them, we'll get the vitamin D we're missing from the sun."

I didn't question her. For weeks, I based all my meals around mushrooms. I made mushroom casseroles, salads, risotto, soups, but I'm not sure it changed me. I'm not sure it changed her. How many mushrooms would it take to replace the sun? I wish I could ask the girl, but she's gone. Three weeks ago, I lost her for good.

I pull up my sleeves and roll up my pants. My arms and legs are so pale in this light. They look like white maps with long blue roads leading to nowhere. The lighting in my house is soft enough to disguise my pallor, but here in the rest home, the deficiency is glaring. I quickly lower my sleeves and pants again. "Focus, Dottie." My command is quiet.

I swallow down one of the tiny white pills and sit up straight in my chair. Pen in hand, I look around the dismal room I currently share with Mario. It is a holding cell for the dying. We aren't dying like the old people in this nursing home. But our town is small. They had nowhere else to put my husband after the accident a decade ago. And they had nowhere else to put me after the devastating incident at my house last week. So now we live together again in room eleven with the beige walls, the brown and yellow floral comforters on our beds, and the slim, dark wood secretary desk beside the bathroom door. The old desk is where I currently sit as I tap my pen on the blank page, trying to gather my thoughts.

Now the cold distracts me. I pull a blanket from the bed and wrap it around me. The air conditioner is dreadfully high. They say it's to keep germs down, but I sometimes wonder if they're trying to weed out the weakest of us.

"Focus, Dottie, focus," I say a little louder, closing my eyes.

"What do you need to focus on?" someone asks.

Startled, I tighten the blanket around me and turn toward the voice. There is a white-haired lady in a wheelchair at my door. Her face is all wrinkled up like fingertips after a long bath, and her lips seem to be growing inward around her teeth. Thick bifocals, wrapped around her head like goggles, magnify her wet and cloudy eyes. There are some really old people here, but she has to be the oldest.

"I didn't mean to frighten you," she says, her ancient voice slowly rattling out the words. "I heard you from the hall."

I wasn't trying to be heard. I place my hand over my mouth to show her I've no interest in a conversation. I'm hoping my hand gesture will make her leave, but it doesn't. Instead, she wheels through the small space between the two beds and parks next to me at the desk. Her nightgown is purple and far too big on her. She smells like leftover broccoli.

"I'm curious. What do you need to focus on?" she asks again. It's going to take some time getting used to this place. I'm not in the habit of answering to anyone, having lived alone for so long.

"A letter," I finally say. She's so close now, there's no escaping her. "I'm writing a letter. A story really. The rumors are terrible and—" I catch myself before it all comes flooding back. Their ugly words. All the lies. "I need to tell my story. It's the only way to get the truth out."

Her face lights up. "You must be Dottie," she whispers. I nod. "I should have known." Her eyes travel the length of me. "I heard about you, the young woman living in the old people's home." It sounds strange out loud but worse things have been said about me. "How old are you, dear?"

"Forty-three."

"So young." She shakes her head. "It's just awful what happened to you. How long will you be staying with us?"

"Well." I look over at Mario in his bed. His eyes are open, but there's no telling what he's thinking as he stares at the ceiling tiles. "The Sisters say I can stay with my husband as long as I need. I've nowhere else to go."

She leans over the side of her chair to get a closer look at him. "Does he even remember who you are?"

"I haven't let a day go by without coming to see him."

"But with what happened to him, do you think he *can* remember?"

"Oh, he remembers me." I won't let anyone convince me otherwise.

"That's nice." Her smile is kind. "Sometimes I think I remember too much," she says. "Some things I wish I could forget, but the pictures are there in my mind, clear as day." She sets her bony hands in her lap, and the veins bulge like soft worms. She smiles. Her demeanor is pleasant; it's just the broccoli smell that's bothersome.

I notice a pin on her nightgown. It's gold with blue letters spelling out CENTENARIAN. I point to it. "You're a hundred?"

"A hundred and two."

"That's incredible," I say, feeling a new respect for her. She's not just an old lady—she's *National Geographic* material.

"It's a curse, old age. The lucky ones die young. Freed from these bodies, they can move on. Or, of course, they can stick around." She raises the few hairs left of her eyebrows, as if I know something about this. I feel her words in my stomach. I don't respond. She whispers, "The ghosts of Sam's Town are persistent, aren't they, Dottie?"

"If you don't mind, I'd like to get back to my letter."

"But we haven't talked about what happened to the girl yet." She laces her fingers together under her chin. "We need to talk about what really happened to Magdalena."

Hearing her name almost makes me lose my breath. I close my eyes and indiscriminate memories resurface—her blue nail polish, those stolen sunglasses on her head, lemon juice dripping from her fingers, her blood on the linoleum.

"Do you know what happened?" the old woman asks. "I mean what *really* happened to her?" She's staring at me, waiting for an answer.

I reach for my pen, gripping it like a weapon. "Until I write it all down, I'm not talking about it to anyone."

"You can trust me, Dottie." She wheels closer.

"I don't even know you," I say.

She smiles. It's a sad smile. "Then let's get to know one another." She glances toward my husband before leaning forward. The smell is strong, her voice is soft. "Is it true that the man," she asks, "who started it all was your lover?"

I close my eyes again, to escape her question, but now there *he* is behind my eyelids—Benjamin. His hand creeps under my dress and he's massaging my leg. I squeeze my eyes tighter.

"Go away!" I shout. "Go away!" I am talking to Benjamin, but when I open my eyes, the old lady in the wheelchair is hunched over, wheeling away as fast as her bony arms will take her. I should explain that I was not yelling at her. But I don't. I stay quiet. While I feel a bit guilty, I'm relieved to see her go.

The poor woman looks so frail heading for the door, like her arms might snap. That's the other effect of vitamin D deficiency—frail bones. This town is killing all of us.

2

The old lady in the wheelchair is gone, but the room still smells like her. I press the red button on the wall beside my bed.

"Yes?" a voice comes through the speaker.

"I had a visitor in my room and she left a smell. It's distracting. Can you bring some kind of deodorizer to get rid of it?" There is a moment of silence. I wonder if I haven't made my problem clear. "It smells like broccoli," I say. "Not freshly cooked broccoli, but broccoli going bad. It was the centenarian lady. Probably just gas, but it's not going away."

"All right, Dottie," the voice crackles through the speaker. I hear someone laughing in the background. It must be one of the high school volunteers, still immature enough to laugh at flatulence. "I'll send someone over right away."

A young man shows up with Pine-Sol spray and douses my room. A quick misting would have solved the problem; now I'm stuck in the overwhelming stench of imitation pine.

"Did you use the whole can?" I ask him.

"No, there's still some left. You want me to spray more?"

"No!" I say quickly. "You've done enough."

"Oh. Too much? Sorry." He rapidly moves the door back and forth, as if that might clear the air. It only makes it worse.

I can't write my letter in here.

For the first time since I moved in with Mario a week ago, I leave our room. Today's unexpected visitor, the one who came before the Centenarian, brought word that someone wants to hear my version of the story. Someone wants me to write down everything that really happened. This request has turned my life upside down—or rather, right side up. I thought the truth would slowly disappear as the townspeople traded ugly tales about me, but now, this opportunity has arisen to dispel the rumors. Of course I'm afraid to tell the truth. It isn't pretty. But at least it shows I am human, not the monster they believe me to be.

I should not care what the people of Sam's Town think of me anymore. They've misunderstood me since I was a young girl. As a child, I loved spending time in my imagination. Sometimes I used the stories I found there to replace the real stories of my life. Like the night my mother left my bedroom window open after climbing out of it to go clear her head. She'd gone through my room so my father wouldn't notice. I told my classmates I left my window open that night to listen to the dolphins and the whales plan a birthday party for a mermaid. I don't know where those silly stories came from, but they thrilled me. And I thought sharing them would thrill the other kids just as much. I was wrong. I spent lunchtime in Sister Rosario's office when the teasing got bad. Even when I stopped telling stories, and eventually stopped talking at school altogether, they continued making fun of me. Their unkind treatment has haunted me all my life and yet here I am, a grown woman, still hopeful that maybe *this time* they will understand me. Like it's a necessity— food, water, air, understanding.

I grab my robe and slippers to keep warm in this meat locker of a place, and head for the door. The mirror on the wall catches me. I stop and touch the reflection. I see my mother's worried eyes and nervous lips. I wear my father in my pale complexion and light brown hair. I'm skinny like my mother, tall like my father. Even my fingertips hold memories of them—the tiny scars are like Mother's signature on me. My parents left town years ago, yet they still creep up on me every now and then. I quickly pull my hands from the mirror and wave their ghosts away.

Stepping from my dimly lit room into the hall, I found the overhead fluorescents piercing. The people in the hall look strange—overexposed like a bad photograph. Glossy, lentil-green floors match the green-and-beige-striped wallpaper. Framed images of the Virgin Mary hang on the walls. These paintings might have an uplifting effect on the old place if not for the sad, elderly people parked beside them, drowsing and drooling in their wheelchairs. There's nowhere they can socialize except the dining room, and it's closed while the staff is preparing lunch and dinner.

It feels like I've been passing the same folks for almost ten years now, although I'm sure some have died and new ones have replaced them. They always look the same. I've tried keeping to myself when I visit Mario, but some are hard to ignore. Old Buck Donenfeld, one of the original fishermen who founded Sam's Town, usually keeps a patch over his missing eye, though sometimes he likes to air it out while lounging in his wheelchair. Henry Smith lost three fingers in an accident at sea and has a habit of rubbing his nubs over his lips while watching the happenings in the hall. Gigi Flowers, once an aspiring actress who used to take a bus to Hollywood auditions, keeps what she has left of her white hair all fluffed up and wears pink lipstick drawn out beyond her lips. She scoots along in her walker telling stories to anyone who will listen. Frail old Natalie Teller, with steel-gray hair and a rash all over her skin, laughs, cries, argues, or chants "Oh no" over and over, depending on what the voices in her head are telling her. It's an eerie place. The rotating doctors see that people are properly medicated. The three Sisters from church, who are also trained nurses, do their best to keep the place clean and respectable, but there's nothing anyone can do about the side effects and indignities of growing old.

At the end of the hall, I slip into the small chapel. It is a dark room with heavy curtains, lit mostly by candlelight—not real candles, a fire hazard, but the flameless kind that run on batteries. A life-size Virgin Mary statue stands on a carpeted base against the wall, and a few wooden benches face the makeshift altar. Most of the room is left open for wheelchairs.

I stay in the back corner where there is a desk with a lamp. The room is empty right now except for one man, asleep in his wheelchair beside the Virgin. His open-mouthed breathing drills into my ears, but I've brought the earplugs Sister Rosario gave to me when I first arrived—in case residents scream in the middle of the night. Sitting at the desk with my blank paper, I put in the earplugs and begin to write.

Dear Ms. McIntosh, I write, addressing my favorite journalist at *Beyond the Veil Magazine.* She believes the things that happened to me would intrigue her readers and she wants to hear my story—my version of it. Everyone in town reads the magazine. This is my chance to explain myself and convince them of my innocence.

I admit I've done some terrible things, but I swear on my life, I swear to all my accusers, I did nothing to harm Magdalena.

3

My letter starts out like a confession. I tell Susan McIntosh how I met Benjamin at the library in Norwood, how I took the bus there at least three days a week, and we sat in room B, enclosed by windows not walls, reading out loud together, each taking five pages at a time. I lived for those days.

It had been about a decade since the accident. A traumatic brain injury left Mario a vegetable. A vegetable. That was the term the doctors used, reducing my once-vibrant husband to a head of cabbage. I resented the insensitivity, but over the long years, I came to understand my husband was no more responsive to me than the produce I bought at Dorado's Market. Even in such a hopeless condition, I'd never had any intention to replace him. I visited him in the rest home every day, and despite being in my early-thirties, I tucked away any desires that surfaced in my still young body and never looked at other men. Romance novels seemed to satiate me, but now I understand I read far too many. My brain was filled with romance, keeping those youthful hormones alive. Following a decade of faithfulness, I finally gave in to temptation.

It began innocently enough between us, two readers at the library who asked for the same book on the same night. With only one copy available, he suggested we share it. Asking how we might do that, he led me to room B and the reading began.

Benjamin looked like he had ancestors from every country. His dark, frizzy hair puffed out when it was short, but fell softly against his shoulders when it grew longer. Tawny skin, deep-set eyes, full lips, and a pointed nose, he was breathtakingly original. He was tall and appeared rather lean under his baggy clothes. Though pleasing to look at, his most attractive feature was his confidence. The outside world might have had a hard time defining him, but he clearly knew who he was.

We were on page forty-two that first night together when I abruptly stood up and straightened my housedress. "I need to go," I told him. I was enjoying myself far too much with this stranger.

"Can we meet here again?" he asked. His eyes, his smile, the tilt of his head, it was all too dreamy for a simple woman like me.

"No. I don't think I can," I said, lowering my eyes and staring down at the beige carpet. "You take the book home. I'll read it when you're done."

"Ah, but it won't be the same." He spoke passionately, a bit too loud. I peeked out the window but no one seemed to have heard. "It was like a duet," he said, "the two of us reading together. Didn't you enjoy hearing it in alternating voices like that?" Keeping my head down, I nodded. "Then can you come Thursday? Or Friday?"

I looked back up at him. "I don't know."

"Okay." He widened that charming smile. "I'll be here Thursday. And Friday. If you decide to come, I'll be waiting."

Wednesday, I told myself I would not go. Thursday, I told myself I should be polite and go back to tell Benjamin I couldn't meet with him so he wouldn't waste his time showing up again on Friday. That was my mistake: trying to be polite.

I write to Susan about how he stood so close to me that day, I could smell him. His scent was clean and strong and somehow deeper than my husband's. Benjamin smelled like nighttime. It's what made me want to stay and continue our reading, and what made me agree to meet again.

I went back to the library to see him again and again in the following months. We grew more comfortable together than we should have. Benjamin held my hand as we read Stephen King novels so I wouldn't get scared, and sometimes while reading love scenes, he put his hand on my bare leg, just under the hem of my dress. We never met in a bedroom, but being together inside a story had its own fever. We never talked about our real lives. He wore a wedding ring like I did, but the fact that he showed up every week told me all I needed to know. We mostly gave our attention to the characters in the books we read, and through them we developed something as passionate as a regular affair.

Desire grew between us. It was a good thing there was no privacy in room B for us to do anything about it. Sometimes as I read, Benjamin leaned in toward me to smell my hair. After a deep inhale, I could hear his breath grow heavy, as if my smell triggered his heart to race. In response my own heart would speed up and make me stutter while reading. His gentle hand on my shoulder, or his soft finger touching my lips, was his way of telling me it was okay to stop for a moment. In the quiet, while we waited for our hearts to calm, he would gaze at me with that dreamy look of his.

I never thought I had it in me to cheat on my husband—but sometimes life throws a Benjamin at you and you can't help but rethink *never*.

After a yearlong relationship, living through all those novels together, Benjamin stopped showing up. We were in the middle of *The Shining* and I knew he was as curious to know the ending as I was. For months, I waited for him to return, visiting the library every day, sitting alone in room B with the windows instead of walls, half reading and half watching for him.

But he never returned. It was all I could think about. He'd given no hint he was tiring of me. In fact the last time we met, he sat especially close and told me our time together was the highlight of his week. Why would he give that up? I came up with several possible reasons for his disappearance, but only one struck me with that intuitive feeling one gets when the truth suddenly reveals itself. Benjamin must have died. He must have!

Once I came to this revelation, I made it my obsession to find Benjamin on the other side. Living in Sam's Town, I knew death didn't mean the end.

ॐ

Mario's Ouija board was in a box in the back of the garage. He and his friends used it when they were kids. I'd never used one. If another ghost showed up in our house, my mother would have had an honest to goodness breakdown. My father kept sage smudge sticks in the same cupboard with the roach spray. Ghosts and roaches never had a chance in our house. They were my mother's two greatest fears. The kids at school bragged about their Ouija board experiences, but I equated playing with one to playing with matches on the carpet. When Mario and I got married and brought our things together, I told him he wasn't allowed to bring the evil game inside.

Loneliness has a way of changing your mind about things. Pushing aside the boxes at the back of the garage, I searched for the board game that seemed far less evil now that I had use for it.

Late at night, I sat on the floor in my living room. With the Ouija board on the coffee table and a lamp lit by the draped window, I called out for Benjamin to come back. Each night I asked him to speak to me through the lettered board as my hopeful fingertips hovered over the planchette. It was exciting to finally engage in ghost business after all my years of avoiding it. Surprisingly, I felt no guilt. My mother was no longer in town so I couldn't hurt her with this. It was time to take care of myself.

Every day for two weeks straight, I called for Benjamin. The planchette slid along the arched alphabet of the magic board, stopping now and then as if a message was trying to come through, but what sometimes felt like guided movement only turned into a jumble of letters. Nothing ever made sense. I wondered if I was doing something wrong.

As a last resort, I simply set the Ouija board on my kitchen table—an open invitation to Benjamin. It took up a lot of space, but I was okay with that. The table was where I might entertain a dinner guest, and the only possible guest I could hope for was Benjamin.

I went back to my ordinary routine. All the while, I did my

best to wear a smile, but it was getting harder. Though losing
Benjamin wouldn't have been the worst of my losses, suffering
one heartbreak after another felt like a gradual tumble down a
cliff. I was about to crash into the ground when the unexpected
happened. Benjamin came through.

4

My letter is five pages long already, and I still haven't told Susan McIntosh about the girl. I set my pen down and close my eyes. Magdalena. I'm afraid ink and paper are not enough for this. If only I'd taken a picture of her while she was still here, or captured some video to remember the way she moved through the world. But I have nothing. Just the story.

I pick up my pen and start at the beginning—the very beginning, before Magdalena and I were born. It's important for Susan to understand this couldn't have happened anywhere else. It only happened because we lived in Sam's Town.

Back in the 1940s three fishing boats pulled into a small bay along a jagged stretch of the Northern Californian coast. Big schools of sardines kept showing up in this area and the fishermen, from the crowded docks of San Francisco, wanted to move closer to the fish. The men climbed up the rocks to an elevated peninsula and found level, spacious land where they could build a small town. Bordered for miles by uneven rocky terrain, the town seemed destined to remain secluded, but they came anyway. Despite its isolation, there was a mysterious charm about the place.

As the first houses were being completed, one of the fisherman's wives, a lady named Samantha, died from the flu. Her spirit stayed in the house her husband had built for her. He said she stood at the foot of his bed each night and watched him fall asleep, which he found comforting, but this ghost made everyone else uneasy. What if her death and constant appearance was a curse on the new settlement? Prone to superstition, the fishermen decided Samantha—or as her husband called her, Sam—would bring no harm to a town named after her. And so they named the place Sam's Town, in honor of the very first ghost that came through.

Over the next decade, workers from nearby wineries and farms came with their families. The neighborhoods filled with tightly packed houses and narrow streets, a simple school for the young and a humble rest home for the old. Soon, there was a market, a café, a bakery, a bar, and a beauty shop on Dorado Avenue, and on the corner of Marlin and Minnow, Saint Mary's by the Sea church. An agreement was made with the town of Norwood, about thirty miles inland, to share its hospital, police, and fire departments, as well as its library, but on a daily basis, Sam's Town was self-reliant. It was a good place to live. And as the community would soon come to learn, it was an even better place to die.

There was never an official explanation on why the dead stayed in Sam's Town. My mother used to say we had an open door to the other side. Most places tried to keep that door shut and even sealed, but ours never closed. Our dead were not forced away, but could return to their loved ones while gradually transitioning to their new conditions. It made living here a strange combination of comforting and unnerving. It was also unusually clarifying. While the rest of the world debated whether or not there was life after death, we knew.

Had we lived in an ordinary city where the living and the dead kept their proper separation, Magdalena and I might have never had reason to meet. Here in Sam's Town we came together because I was looking for a ghost, and she knew how to find him.

Magdalena lived next door to me with her grandmother, an unpleasant old lady called Buttons. Buttons was a seamstress, the person everyone in town went to for alterations or repairs, and she was also the Sunday school teacher. Whenever a child misbehaved, she would sew a red or black button on the front of his or her shirt. After the child repented, she would rip the button off instead of cutting it, leaving a hole in the fabric. In that way, the naughty kids could easily be identified until they outgrew their holey shirts.

I'd been so afraid of Buttons as a child that I initially told Mario I couldn't handle living next door to her. But this was the only available house on the peninsula. Since people here rarely moved away, we would have been forced to move to Norwood.

Surprisingly, the old lady didn't bother us. She was friendly enough with Mario as he had a way of bringing out the best in people, and since I always lowered my eyes in her presence, she came to ignore me. Later, when Magdalena arrived, Buttons was consumed with the unexpected responsibility of having to raise a grandchild. I never had a problem living beside her and her granddaughter until a knock on my door broke our two decades of peace.

The air that day was thick and fishy. Sometimes the ocean exhaled from deep within its belly, leaving the stench to linger in the fog. I opened my front door to the ocean's pungent breath and standing there was the neighbor girl I'd never spoken to before. I'd only seen her from a distance. Up close, I discovered how uncommonly beautiful fifteen-year-old Magdalena had become. Her long cinnamon hair, which just about reached her waist, framed the flower that was her face. She had big brown lonely eyes, the prettiest little nose, and full, careless lips. Her warm brown complexion was flawless. I couldn't pull my eyes away.

She wore a bright paisley mini-dress with flared sleeves and a peace patch ironed over her heart. Most people in town could only afford to buy their clothes at Norwood's Goodwill, where the racks held clothes for decades. A hippie's dress that might have been worn to an antiwar protest now hung, outdated and frivolous, on the pretty small-town girl.

"Hi," she said, holding up a plastic bag filled with lemons. "Our tree is full and my grandma asked me to give some to the neighbors. Since we'll never use them all."

"She asked you to bring them to *me*?"

"Well, you're a neighbor."

"But I don't think she meant for you to bring them to me,"
I tried to explain.

"They're just lemons. She doesn't care who I give them to."
It was clear Magdalena didn't understand the way things
were. I was oil to the town's water. No amount of stirring would
ever make me blend, and we'd all come to accept the natural
separation. Exclude, ignore, dismiss. Everyone understood the
arrangement. Except, apparently, this girl at my door.

"Do you want them or not?" She raised the bag again, her
wide paisley sleeve cascading down her arm.

"All right." I almost smiled. "I'll take them." I reached for
the bag, but she suddenly drew it close to herself.

"Let me carry them in for you." She tilted her head toward
the open space between the door and me, as if to peek inside
my house.

"That's not necessary. I can carry them."

"The bag's kind of heavy, though," she said, still trying to
see inside.

"It's nice of you to offer." I pulled the door to meet my
shoulder. "But I can manage."

She stared at me, her eyes honest and eager. "I'll just come
in for a minute."

Her persistence made me uncomfortable. I hadn't had a
visitor in years. I didn't know how to be a host, how to carry a
conversation, or how to ask her to leave when the time came.
"No," I told her.

She gave an exasperated sigh. "Okay, I will walk them in and
set them on your counter, and then go. That's it. I'll literally just
carry them in for you and then leave."

"I can carry them just fine."

Magdalena continued to stare, as if thinking how else she
might convince me. I stared back.

"Okay, here," she finally said handing me the bag. "Just take
'em." She didn't seem mad. More disappointed.

"Thank you," I said as the girl in the outdated dress scurried
down the sidewalk back to her house.

The whole episode was curious. Why would a girl like that want to come into my house? Was she at odds with her friends and family, and needed someone to lend an ear? I knew enough of her scandalous family history, and why she had come to live with her grandmother, to understand a little about the things that might trouble her. Not being privy to town gossip anymore without Mario around, I could only assume her family dramas had escalated. Was it callous of me to turn her away?

It was too late to question my decision. The girl was gone. Instead I focused on my gift of lemons.

Taking a knife to one of the lemons, I cut it open and squeezed the first half into a glass. The aroma was fresh and citrusy, a pleasing smell to replace the day's fishy air. "Ave Maria" came to my mind, and I began humming the Latin hymn since I didn't know all the words. The song reminded me of funerals, and yet it gave me a happy feeling that afternoon.

While I was squeezing the second half of the lemon into the glass, my kitchen lights dimmed. The knife fell to the floor, just missing my foot. I stopped humming.

"Benjamin?"

The kitchen was quiet. Everything was still, and yet suddenly cold, the kind of cold Father Candido warned us about. Goosebumps covered my skin. I could feel someone there with me. I might have been scared had I not known it was the kind and gentle Benjamin. Picking up the knife, I kept my head down so he wouldn't see me blushing.

Self-conscious in his sudden presence, I smoothed down my hair and continued making lemonade, like I would have for a regular visitor. Now that he was finally here, I didn't know what to say. I started to hum again, hoping he would somehow initiate the communication, but he didn't. He just quietly stayed with me.

I took out the sugar and opened my utensil drawer for a stirring spoon. The kitchen light spilled into the drawer, and three silverfish went wiggling away to the corners. Those strange little bugs lived in every room of my house, feeding on my books, magazines, wallpaper, drapes, photographs, and even clothes. Spotting them always put me in an unpleasant mood, but I didn't want Benjamin to see me that way. I caught one of the scurrying bugs and pressed it between my fingers until I squeezed the life out of it. At the sink, I washed the tiny corpse from my hand. Usually I would remove the drawer and search for the escapees, but this time I let them go.

I carried two glasses of lemonade to the table and set them beside the Ouija board. My chair faced the narrow galley kitchen—its flat white cupboards, pale pink-tiled counters, the brown-and-beige-flecked linoleum floor, and the glass-louver window over the sink. Each time I took a sip, I glanced around, waiting for Benjamin to appear or at least move something again. He never did. But I felt him. Along with the chill, there was a thickness of energy taking up space in the room—that feeling you get when someone's behind you, before you turn to see who it is.

Benjamin stayed long enough for me to finish my glass, a rather polite gesture I thought, but then he was gone. I could feel the emptiness in the house again. He hadn't stayed for long, but he came. And I knew he would be back.

5

The man sleeping in the wheelchair beside the Virgin appears to be having a violent dream. My earplugs are no match for his yelling. Sister Mary Margaret and Sister Mary Ann come in to the chapel to help him, but the young, inexperienced nuns smile and tap him as if gentle kindness is all that's needed. If Sister Rosario were here, or the two ancient nuns who'd finally retired and given these young ladies a job, they would have used a full-body grab to bring him back into his skin. Instead, the sweet nuns continue tapping him and talking to him in their singsong voices. It doesn't work.

I gather up my pages and leave the chaos.

Keeping my head down in the hall, I begin to reread what I've written. My eyes are on my words so I don't see her right away. But I smell her. The Centenarian is in her wheelchair, following behind me, keeping some distance. I wonder if she's afraid of me now.

"I didn't mean to yell at you earlier," I say, wrapping my arms around my robe to keep warm. "I was actually talking to someone else in my mind. It just came out wrong."

She smiles. "You never know which ones are crazy around here."

"Oh, I can assure you I'm not crazy." I keep walking. She keeps wheeling, right beside me. That word makes the itching in my scalp flare up, just above my left ear. I dig my nail into the spot and scratch it before it gets worse.

With the old houses crowded together on Anchovy Avenue, it was easy listening in on the sidewalk gossip from my front window. All I had to do was lie on the floor under the window or tuck myself into the drapes and the sound of their voices carried right to me. When they hid behind one of the trees, or were lost in a thick fog, I could still hear them. That's how I learned what my neighbors thought of me. They nicknamed me Odd Dottie and they called me crazy. It was the kind of crazy they were willing to tolerate, until the incident with Magdalena turned the entire town against me. Misunderstood—that's what I am. But I am *not* crazy.

"Did you finish the letter?" the old lady asks when we reach the door to my room. Buck Donenfeld is across the hall, watching us with one eye. Natalie Teller is beside him. She is laughing at something on the ceiling.

"Finish? I barely started."

"But you were in there writing a long time."

"It's not a simple letter. This could take days and days. Weeks even."

"Hmm." She adjusts her bifocals with a shaky hand. "Do you think you can be quicker about it?"

I raise my eyebrows. "Quicker? I'm going to write this at my own pace," I tell her, backing into my room while still facing her.

"But I should warn you, dear, the sooner you get it done, the better."

My itching has crawled down my neck. The tiny white pills are supposed to ease my anxiety, but this one symptom still comes through. Turning my back to her, I toss my pages on the bed and grab the cortisone cream from the nightstand. I rub it into my scalp and neck, knotting my hair at the roots. I sit on the edge of Mario's bed and rhythmically scratch with both hands, waiting for the itching to ease.

"Your story is an important one," the old lady says as she enters my room. The faded daylight outside breaks through the curtains just enough to outline the tiny figure in the wheelchair.

"Why is *my story* important to *you*?" I ask, sounding snottier than I'd intended. I feel like I'm back in fifth grade, on the playground. The Sisters encouraged me to join the hopscotch tournament, but the two Lisas and Jennifer were terrorizing me again.

Dottie's mom, Dottie's mom, sitting in jail,
she can't come home 'cause she can't post bail.

It was true my mother was taken to the police station in Norwood for questioning, but the police didn't send her to jail. My father showed up, explained her confusion, and the police released her. The two Lisas and Jennifer didn't know about mental illness. They didn't understand my mother was not bad, just confused. And so they used my family as part of their rhymes whenever my mother made it into the town's gossip.

"The girl knows things," the Centenarian says, bringing me back to the present. "She's special. The people in town need to know she's special. She doesn't deserve what happened to her." Her silhouette is small and hunched, yet there is something commanding about her presence.

"What do you think happened to her?"

"Something terrible," she says, and I realize she must believe the rumors. "She's just a child, but she's the only one who understands the mysteries of the dead. Everyone else here has been taught to fear them."

Clearly, she knows Magdalena. "Did she help you with a ghost?" I whisper. My scratching is slower and gentler. The cream is beginning to work.

"She did," the Centenarian says. Her palms are upturned, her old fingers curled like they're holding something.

"Here? At the rest home?"

"No. It was before I came here."

The woman is a hundred and two and the girl is fifteen. Confused, I ask, "How long ago?"

The Centenarian grips her wheels and slowly maneuvers her chair to face me. Her mouth turns up in a smile so wide her eyes get lost as she says, "She was only five. She shouldn't have known what to do, but she understood the link between the living and the dead as if she'd lived lifetimes before this one."

It is eerily quiet. The old woman holds her smile and keeps her eyes on me. I scoot back on Mario's bed. My weight is pressing down on his leg, but he is unfazed.

"Who did she help you contact?"

"My daughter."

"I'm sorry," I say, understanding.

"Don't be. They all die sometime." Her callousness is unsettling, but I imagine at her age death is easier to accept.

She hesitates as if there is more she wants to say. She opens her mouth and the beginning of a word comes out, but then she closes her lips and shakes her head. As she wheels herself toward the door, I hear her say, "She's not ready yet. All in its proper time. All in its proper time."

6

He came whenever I cut lemons. Each morning, just before sunrise, I squeezed a fresh lemon in a glass, and when the smell rose up, Benjamin came.

The morning after the knife fell from the cutting board, a freshly cut lemon triggered the kitchen lights to flicker for at least ten seconds. The next morning, the alarm on the stove went off, and the toaster slid down and popped up without my touching it. There were footsteps some days, or a light scratching on the walls, and sometimes he opened a door or a cabinet. Sure, I was a little jumpy, but the excitement it brought to my otherwise predictable life made me embrace his gentle haunting.

One night at dinner, I squeezed a wedge of lemon onto my baked chicken and the television peppered on. I ran into the living room to find the picture on the old Zenith screen uncharacteristically clear. Usually it only worked when I balled up aluminum foil on the antenna to hold the reception. Otherwise the picture turned to static. A remarkably vivid scene of the newsman recounting the day's crimes showed me how strong Benjamin's spirit was.

With each sign from him, I would say his name. But then he would go away. At least it seemed like he went away. I wondered if he was up in the ceiling, quietly watching me, or if death has a world of its own and Benjamin left me each morning to go explore. His absence mystified me, but not his return. Lemons always brought him back.

Magdalena had given me enough lemons to last five days. On a Tuesday, while I was cleaning up my dinner dishes, I realized the bag was empty. I worried I might not get a visit from Benjamin the next morning. From my kitchen window, I could see that Magdalena's tree still had plenty of fruit, and they were almost within reach from my yard.

Dusk gave me just enough light to pull Mario's old ladder from our detached garage. Leaning the ladder against the fence, I climbed up three steps and peeked into Magdalena's backyard. No lights, no movement, no sounds, just the bell buoy off in the distance, clanging the uneasy melody of Sam's Town.

Stepping up another rung, I was able to reach the tree. Quietly I dropped lemons into the plastic bag hung from my shoulder. Leaves rattled as I plucked the lemons from their branches.

"You could've just asked. I would've brought more over."

I jumped at the unexpected voice in the dim light. Trying to calm my racing heart, I scanned the darkened yard. She was in the corner, by the back gate that led to the alley, sitting on the ground beside a stack of firewood.

"Magdalena?"

"Yeah," she said. "It's just me."

"You scared me." I dropped the plastic bag down to my wrist and hid my loot behind the fence. "I used all the lemons already," I told her. "I didn't have any more—I didn't think you'd mind if—"

"It's fine. You're welcome to all the lemons you need."

"Thank you." I cleared my throat. "I've grown accustomed to having lemonade every night, and when I ran out—"

"You don't have to explain." She got up and walked across the yard. Standing below me, she gripped the top of the wooden fence. "Let's be honest," she said. "I'm guessing the lemons worked. They brought back whoever it is you're trying to contact."

How could she possibly know this? I thought.

As if she'd read my mind, she said, "Your front drapes don't close all the way. I saw you with the Ouija board."

My heart quickened and I had to grip the ladder for stability. "I've never used one before," I whispered. "I'm not that kind of woman. I only tried it for a specific person—I had no other way to—"

"Don't worry." She cut off my explanation. "I won't tell anyone. Actually," she whispered, "I can help you."

"How?" I asked.

She looked back at her house, and then went up on her toes as she whispered again, "I'm a sensitive."

I narrowed my eyes. "What's a sensitive?"

"I can see them and hear them." Going higher on her toes, she said, "I communicate with the other side."

7

On a map, the Sam's Town peninsula looks like a finger pointing out toward the open sea. Along the sides of the finger, cliff tops with long narrow stretches of grass, trees, and walkways comprise the Northside Park and the Southside Park. At the very tip, eight houses once enjoyed the only oceanfront view in town. It seemed a lucky place to live, there on Cod Avenue, high above the water with front row seats to the Pacific Ocean, until a major earthquake struck in the late sixties. The cliffs shook with the force of Almighty God, as my mother used to say, then gave way and plunged into the water. Those eight houses cracked open like eggs, spilling lives into the ocean below. It took two days to find all twenty-seven bodies.

I was just four, but I remember the town's grief. We all went to Mass twenty-seven days straight—a funeral for each of the dead. Everyone wore black, and a black station wagon with maroon curtains came at the end of each funeral to take away the casket. We followed the station wagon down the narrow streets on those drizzly days, to the end of Dorado Avenue, where the peninsula meets the mainland. From under the trees, we watched the black car take the two-lane highway up around the mountain and disappear.

Those nights after the funerals, my father stayed at the table and worked on a drawing of the black station wagon while my mother did dishes. When he had his sketchpad open, I had to leave him alone. I was allowed to peek quietly over his shoulder as long as I didn't say a word. That was the only way I ever glimpsed what was in his mind.

Immersed in his art, my father never noticed the way my mother dried the steak knives on her long sleeves instead of the dishtowel. I watched her wipe them on the material over her wrists with graceful slicing motions, as if the knives were props in some kind of dance. As a child, I loved watching the strange things my mother did. I could tell she lived in more worlds than just the one we shared. I thought they were magical worlds. Following the last funeral, in an after-dinner dance with a knife, my mother sliced her wrist. My father borrowed a neighbor's car, drove us to the Norwood Hospital, and left my mother there. The hospital transported her to a special ward in San Francisco, where she stayed for a month with other patients who'd tried to kill themselves. As the rest of the town stopped wearing black and began pulling out of their mourning, I fell into a sadness thicker than the fog. I hadn't known anyone who died in the landslide, but losing my mother for the month felt like a kind of death.

During her absence, I went to the church preschool while my father went to work. I waited by the window the entire day until my father came to get me. He was the accountant at the same winery, owned by the Catholic church, where Mario would one day work. They let him leave by three each afternoon, and when he got home, he took me for a walk to the edge of town. There at the broken cliffs, we stood side by side, silently taking in the scene behind the recently erected concrete barriers and chain-link fences. Like my mother, my father seemed to have another world inside his head, but I never thought his was magical. My father was a thinker. Sometimes he thought so deeply he forgot the people around him. Those afternoons, he never noticed me placing my hands over my eyes when we stayed too long.

Only the fronts of the eight houses remained—sunken, cracked, lopsided, detached. It was cartoonish, the way the once pretty houses were broken into halves with nothing but a drop to the ocean behind them. Below the yellow warning signs was a homemade shrine that spanned the entire chain-link fence: Virgin Mary statues, crosses, saint figurines, rosaries, framed prayer cards, and flowers, placed there by our friends and neighbors. Closer to the houses, lawn chairs lay on their backs. A Big Wheel sat beside one of the unhinged front doors, and a scattering of bikes, gardening tools, and potted plants told unfinished stories.

It felt like punishment, standing there taking in the destruction that had killed twenty-seven people. I could only close my eyes and pretend I was somewhere else since I wouldn't dare ask to leave. I took myself to faraway San Francisco, in a room that had flowers and birds, and my mother danced with a feather in her hand instead of a knife. There I stayed, watching my happy mother, until my father pulled me from the fantasy.

Once he'd seen enough at the cliffs, he'd walk me back home and spend hours drawing segments of the horrible scene in his sketchpad. He did this every day until my mother returned.

She never said a word about her hospital stay. She spoke only about the news she'd read in the newspaper throughout the month—the obituaries, the geological reports that declared the rest of the peninsula safe, the plans to clean up the mess, the lack of funds that would postpone those plans. The concoction of pills she now took made her less of a dreamer and more like my father. This lasted a couple months, until she refused to take the pills any longer, but for that short time, the three of us hovered on the verge of happiness. Even my father showed some uncharacteristic optimism in his otherwise bleak sketchbook.

Upon her return, she was the subject of my father's next drawing, smiling and glowing, standing beside new houses on the cliffs. The houses were whole, upright and prettier than the ones before. It lifted me out of my sadness. I imagined seeing Sam's Town healthy again. Unfortunately, that vision never came to pass—for the town or for my mother.

City officials from Norwood promised to come out and clean up the mess once the earth stabilized, but now, over forty years later, the temporary barriers have become familiar enough to seem normal, and those promises are long forgotten. Nothing has been repaired. The broken houses are left to the mercy of the elements. Invasive morning glory has wrapped around the debris. Tall weeds grow in the spaces between the houses and the fences and cover the old shrine, now molded beyond recognition. Two pine trees, at the edge of the crumbled cliff, still hang on by their roots and grow at awkward slants. Rats have taken up residence in the cliffside jungle, but they are not the only occupants left on the broken edge of town.

When the station wagon with the maroon curtains took away the bodies of the dead, their spirits did not leave. There had been ghosts passing through since the town began, but nothing like the surge of hauntings that came after the landslide. Father McKenzie got calls from parishioners almost every day complaining about "spiritual disturbances." He visited house after house, trying to pray the ghosts away. But the ghosts seemed determined to stay. After months of failure, Father McKenzie asked the archdiocese to transfer him to another church and give the people of Sam's Town a more qualified priest.

Father Candido was a serious man with an expertise in exorcisms. He had a freckly face, suspicious, bulging eyes, and an unusually wide mouth. As a five-year-old, I thought the new priest looked like a frog. I told my mom and at first she laughed but then she slapped me. Following her time in the suicide ward, she became unpredictable like that.

My mom didn't like Father Candido, but she respected him. He did seem to have a way with ghosts, and within a year of his arrival, the landslide hauntings were under control. While everything else about my mom was falling apart, her home finally had some stability.

Late at night when my mom couldn't sleep, she'd crawl into my bed, not wanting to wake my father with her restlessness, and retell me a story she couldn't seem to get out of her mind.

"Just after sunset, behind the chain-link fence, the smells and sounds of their old lives rose up," she whispered. I could barely see her, but I knew her eyes were storytelling-wide. "The smells of dinners and cigars drifted into nearby neighborhoods. The sounds of children playing and adults laughing. We all heard them trying to recapture their old lives. Their deaths were too abrupt. They didn't understand what had happened. They thought they still belonged here."

"And they wandered through town," I said, having memorized her story.

My mother rolled away from me, her head flat on the pillow as she faced the ceiling. "You're getting ahead of me." She was upset, no longer whispering. She'd always let me join in and recite the parts I knew. I didn't know why this time I'd made her angry. "I'm trying to tell the story and you're ruining it. Do you want to tell it? Should I just stop so you can tell it?"

"No. I'm sorry. You tell it, Mom."

"But I've lost my place now. I've lost my train of thought. I might as well go sleep on the couch," she said, getting up.

"They wandered through town and one came to our house," I told her, reaching for her arm. "That's the next part. When one of them came to our house. Please, Mom, stay and tell me the story."

She took a few sharp breaths through her nose. "If you don't interrupt me again."

"I won't. I promise."

She lay back down and adjusted her head on the pillow. "I was lying in bed," she whispered again, "and I felt an invisible pressure, as if someone were sitting on me." Under the covers, she put her hand on my stomach and pressed hard. She'd never done that before. I tolerated the uncomfortable feeling so she would continue, but she pressed harder. She was testing me. Would I interrupt her again? I didn't react. "The air was cold and I knew someone was in the room with me. I knew it was one of the ghosts from the landslide," she said, now using both hands. I tried to steady my breathing. I tried to avoid making a sound, but I couldn't take it anymore. I had to cough to catch my breath. That was when she let go. I had a feeling it was more than a test. It was my punishment. Now she was satisfied.

"We were ready to move away from Sam's Town," she said, jumping ahead. She'd left out all the other ghost encounters around town, but I didn't correct her. "In fact, more than half of the town was preparing to move. A massive exodus was just about underway when the great miracle of Sam's Town changed everything."

It was one of my favorite parts of the story. The way she told it, I usually got chills, but this time I was distracted. My stomach still hurt. My breathing felt strained. I had to cough, and though I managed to make the first one quiet, the ones that followed were fast and loud. That was the last straw for my mother.

"Now I've completely lost my place." She got out of my bed. "My head is too full. I can't concentrate with all your noise." She left my room without finishing the story.

Her head was too full. I knew what that meant—she was on the verge of a breakdown. I would tell my father the next morning and our goal for the day would be finding a way to get her to take her medication.

"Father McKenzie left," I whispered, trying to finish the story myself. "And Father Candido came to replace him."

I closed my eyes. The story wasn't the same without my mom. I couldn't get myself to retell the great miracle without her lying there beside me. And without the miracle, there was no sense retelling the next part of the story, how Father Candido expelled most of the ghosts. Nor did I give voice to his warning about the few remaining ghosts he hadn't been able to drive out—that they would only enter the houses of those not in a state of grace. It wasn't like the old days when a ghost was just a visitor—now it became a sign of sinfulness. That was my least favorite part of the story. Shame and secrecy overtook the town as neighbors told on other neighbors when they suspected ghost activity next door.

But no one had to tell on my mother when a ghost showed up at our house. She called the new priest herself.

While the gossip that circulated after Father Candido came to our house was bad, what I witnessed that night was worse. An exorcism was not the standard approach to dealing with ghosts, but Father Candido believed that those not in a state

of grace had succumbed to wayward spirits. And as an expert
in such matters, we trusted him. My mother slept for four days
straight after what the priest did to her. The ghost was gone,
but the stigma of his visit remained.

In my mother's late-night stories, Father Candido never
came to our house. He rid the town of most of its ghosts, but
not the one in our house. She took out that disgraceful detail
and replaced it with something better. It was my father, armed
with fresh sage sticks, who cleansed our home of the ghost.
And it was my obedience and my nightly prayers that kept us in
God's good graces so the ghost wouldn't return. We were the
heroes of the story.

The more times I heard my mother's version, the closer
I came to believing it—the closer I came to forgetting what
really happened. But the night she left me without giving me
the better ending, I lay alone in my bed with the truth. As the
memory of Father Candido replayed over and over, my fears
grew into little monsters who promised the old priest would
one day come for me. Petrified, I vowed to forever stay in God's
graces so a ghost could never enter a house where I lived.

8

She knew what the lemons could do. It wasn't common knowledge. The girl must have had some experience with the other side. So I let her in.

Magdalena walked barefoot on my living room carpet, her toenails painted blue. It was a weekday and she still wore her school uniform, the same one I'd worn as a girl at Saint Mary's by the Sea High School—navy and white plaid skirt hemmed just above the knee and a white collared shirt. A wooden rosary hung from her neck that she mindlessly wrapped and unwrapped around her fingers.

Magdalena was at that age where she teetered between girl and woman. Her legs were rather graceless, as if adjusting to their new length, yet her blossoming hips moved with the knowledge of who she was to become. I remembered the age. I remembered the feeling. Though I was not blessed with that kind of beauty, there was something familiar about being fifteen.

Magdalena looked around, still fidgeting with the rosary. Her attention breathed new life into the small, dimly lit living room. It made me feel like I was also seeing it for the first time—the orange velvet couch and matching love seat, the Zenith television with built-in cabinet speakers, the painting on the wall featuring a girl in a red dress, the gold and glass bookshelf, a small red paisley chair by the window. Most of our furnishings were from the Goodwill in Norwood, since Mario didn't make enough to buy new furniture at Sears. He found the painting at a yard sale for just a few dollars, and I found the red paisley chair sitting in front of a house on Minnow with a sign that said $10. The chair didn't quite go with the orange couches, but I couldn't pass it up for that price. It had a small rip in the seat that gave my nervous fingers a place to hide while sitting at the window.

Magdalena let the rosary drop to her chest. She sat down on

the couch and began to pet the orange velvet as if it were a dog. I sat on the loveseat across from her and folded my hands in my lap. "I don't want you to be afraid of me," she finally said. "Or afraid of what I do." She stopped petting the couch and took hold of the rosary again. She wrapped and unwrapped the wooden beads with a one-two-three, one-two-three rhythm as she kept her steady eyes on me. "I'm completely normal except I can see and talk to ghosts."

I was slightly afraid of her, but not enough to send her away. "Okay," I said.

"And don't be afraid of them either. They're just like regular people. Except they're dead." I nodded. "Do you have any questions before we start?"

"Um, yes. I have a question," I said, sitting forward in my seat. "How old were you when you first saw one?"

"I've always seen them. I thought everyone did." She pulled her long legs up to the couch and folded them beneath her like a pretzel. "When I was younger, no one understood why I wandered around and ended up in people's houses or in their backyards. I didn't go there on my own. The ghosts led me there, usually to give a message to someone. But when I passed the messages on, no one believed me. They thought I was trouble, like my mother." She pulled her legs all the way up to her chest and hugged her arms around them, chin on her knees. The rosary swayed from side to side like a hypnotist's watch. I stared at it, leaning forward into the girl's spell until she broke it with the question. "Did you know my mother?"

I pulled back, flustered. "No."

"Did you ever see her?"

"I don't remember. She left town when I was so young."

She narrowed her eyes. "But you've heard about her."

What could I say? Everyone in Sam's Town had heard about her. In a small town where gossip is gold, Magdalena's mother was a treasure chest.

They called her Maggie. It was short for Magdalena. The two shared the name. The second Magdalena, the one in my living room, came to town with some new-age name, like Indigo or Serenity, but Buttons quickly changed it to the same name she'd used for her own daughter. It was as if she was being given a second chance to get right what she'd previously gotten wrong.

The story went that Maggie was a drunk. She'd somehow raised a son through her drunkenness, only to end up pregnant once he'd grown. Her adult son kept an eye on her mothering, knowing from his own difficult childhood that she wasn't good at it. One day he found her passed out drunk while his sister cried alone in the crib. So he took the baby to Sam's Town and asked his estranged grandmother to give his sister a better upbringing than he'd had. Buttons, my pious neighbor, couldn't say no, especially with other neighbors right there on the sidewalk gaping at the strange tattooed young man at her door. She agreed to take the child on the condition that her daughter and grandson keep their corrupt lives away from her and the baby.

After the arrival of baby Magdalena, details of Maggie's sordid life in Hollywood spread throughout town. She was a psychic, a mind reader. She reached inside people's thoughts with the help of demons, and she'd raised her son to practice his own brand of black magic. It was said he healed people by promising their souls to the devil. Over the years, the stories of sin and depravity continued—living in seedy motels, organizing séances, an affair with a married man, different men fathering her children. The second Magdalena had no chance at a clean slate with that kind of history behind her.

"Don't believe what you've heard." Magdalena was firm. "The people around here are too small-minded to understand someone like my mother. I won't be able to help you if you're small-minded like them."

I kept my hands in tight fists in my lap. "I'm not like the rest of the people here."

"Good." She smiled—just half a smile really, only one side of her mouth lifted. "Neither am I."

For the first time being an outcast felt like a good thing and I smiled too.

She untangled her long legs and set her bare feet back on the floor. "As long as you don't think like them, I can help you." The girl stood up and went to the front window. There was a slight gap in the drapes where the material didn't meet. She tried closing it, but it wouldn't stay, so she held it closed with her hand as she asked, "Does your ghost have a name?"

I nodded. "Benjamin."

"Why are you trying to contact Benjamin?"

I didn't know what to say. I couldn't tell this young girl that I, a married woman, had a relationship with another man.

"Don't worry," she said, as if reading my mind. "I'm very discreet. With all my clients."

"Your clients?" I asked. "So you do this for money?"

"If I did it for free, people would take advantage of me."

"But what do you charge?"

She let go of the drapes and went to the bookshelf behind me. I twisted around in my seat to watch her. With her back to me, she said, "Fifty dollars a session."

"Fifty dollars!" I placed my hand over my heart. "You didn't mention in the backyard this would cost anything. I don't have that kind of money."

She ran her finger down the spines of a few paperbacks as she tilted her head to read the titles. I could see her fingernail polish had peeled down to what looked like small pink amoebas, unlike the fresh blue coat on her toes. When she'd finished with the books, she stepped toward the painting. Standing before it, she stared at the girl in the red dress for some time.

"Okay," she finally said. "For you, I'll do it for twenty-five." She turned to me and asked, "Can you afford that?"

I thought about the money I had hidden in my sock drawer for emergencies. This wasn't quite an emergency, and yet I considered it urgent. Benjamin was dead. He could move on at any time.

"What exactly do you do?" I asked.

The confidence in her young eyes was breathtaking. "Instead of telling you, let me show you."

9

In the kitchen, Magdalena turned off the lights and lit candles—three on the counter, and one on the Ouija board. The girl grabbed her long hair and twisted it round and round until the great mass was piled into a bun atop her head. Somehow she tucked in the ends so that it stayed in place. It looked like a bird's nest, one a great priestess might wear.

The young priestess turned to the cutting board and cut one of the lemons I'd pulled from the tree. Holding half in each hand, she walked to the table and opened her arms. Lifting her chin, eyes toward the ceiling, she called out, "Benjamin, we invite you in." She squeezed the lemon. A touch of juice sprayed out while the rest dripped through her fingers onto my floor. I briefly considered grabbing a wet towel to wipe it up, but I resisted and forced myself back into the moment.

The kitchen was silent but for the refrigerator's soft hum. Through the flickering candlelight, I watched the lemon juice continue to drip onto the linoleum. A chill began to overtake the room, and as I wrapped my arms around myself, a rush of air grazed me, as if someone had walked by. Magdalena followed with her eyes. My heart sped up. Benjamin had been visiting me each day, but this time we were joined by a real sensitive. I backed to the counter and held onto the pink tiles for support.

"Do you see him?" I whispered.

"Yes," she whispered back with the calm of one who had seen enough ghosts not to be afraid anymore.

The air was chilly and still. Magdalena pointed to a drawer and gave a slight nod. It slowly opened. Once it had opened all the way, she nodded again and it slammed shut. I gasped at the sudden sound, slapping my hand over my mouth. The girl gave that half smile, and then moved to the window over the sink. She pointed to the lever that controlled the glass louvers and nodded again. Slowly the lever turned by itself and the panels separated, opening the window. Cool ocean air blew into the kitchen, along with the faint sound of the bell buoy. With another nod, the lever traveled the opposite way until the window was closed. She nodded toward the sink, and the water turned on. The same command turned it off. Up on her toes she spun around, her plaid skirt widening like a parasol, and the back door behind us slammed shut. I jumped. I hadn't realized it was open.

"Don't worry," she whispered. "I told him to."

I wasn't actually worried, just surprised. I knew Benjamin was too kind to cause any harm. Fear was not the emotion I felt there in my kitchen. I was in awe. In a town overwhelmed by the mysteries of our lingering dead, here was a girl who understood them.

With her back to me, Magdalena whispered something to Benjamin, though I couldn't hear what she said. Her body language was at ease with the man only she could see and hear. I watched her every move, from the way she toyed with her rosary to the way she balanced on one bare foot while the other mindlessly grazed her calf. She was fidgety, her long limbs loose like spaghetti. I found her fascinating and could have watched her all day.

She set both feet back on the ground and pointed to the kitchen table. In what seemed to be the finale of her act, the table began to tremble. It lifted up on one side, and then the other, as it hovered slightly above the ground. The Ouija board and candle slid toward the floor, but Magdalena caught the candle with one hand and steadied the board with the other. She pushed the table back to the ground. Turning to me she asked, "Was that enough?"

"That was incredible," I whispered. She gave a nod.

"Now it's time to send you on your way," she called out. With a sweep of her hand, high above her head, she firmly said, "Benjamin? Be gone!"

The session with Benjamin was over. The room slowly regained its warmth, and yet I remained in a trance—not only because of the ghost who had come to my house, but because of the girl who was still there.

Magdalena turned the lights back on, blew out the candles, and sat with me at the table. She told me there was so much more she could do, but she needed to know if I was interested in hiring her. What I'd witnessed was absolutely miraculous. Almost equally miraculous was this girl in my home.

My heart begged me to say yes, but my mind considered the risk. Making contact with a ghost was taboo in Sam's Town. I was willing to call for Benjamin on my own, but involving the girl was playing with fire. Buttons, the most intimidating woman in town, was her grandmother, and she lived right next door. If she caught us, there was no telling what she would do.

There at the table, Magdalena pressed me for an answer.

"But what if your grandmother finds out?" I asked.

"Don't be afraid of her. She's just a mean lady." For the first time, the mysterious girl sounded like a sassy teenager. "She pretends to be so righteous but she's no saint." She let her head drop toward her shoulder and lifted her eyebrows in such a way I knew she was about to share some gossip. "At seven o'clock every night, my grandma takes a bottle of wine to her room and watches the Jesus channel until she passes out."

"Buttons?" I said, my hand over my mouth.

She nodded vigorously. "My mother's not the only drunk in the family. She's just the only honest one." Magdalena leaned her elbows on the table. "But you can't tell anyone. If you do, my grandma will make your life miserable."

"I won't," I said. "I won't say a word."

She sat back in the chair and unraveled her bun. Her long cinnamon hair spilled down over her shoulders and she shook her head to help it settle. Watching her, I ran my fingers through my flat, shoulder-length hair, wondering what life felt like for beautiful girls.

"So do you want me to come back again?" she asked. "I'll make sure my grandma doesn't know. You don't have to worry about getting caught."

Breathless and lost in a million thoughts, half of which did not even concern Benjamin, I said yes.

10

There is a knock at the door. "Dottie?"

"Yes," I say, jumping up from my bed, turning the letter face down.

A teenage boy walks in, wearing a striped shirt the high school volunteers wear. He is tall and wispy, his tight black jeans accentuating how little he must eat. Light facial hair sprouts from his otherwise baby-looking face—little soft brown hairs that are not yet manly enough to be called a mustache. He's holding a blue Styrofoam box filled with mushrooms.

"They told me to bring this to you."

"Oh?" I narrow my eyes.

"They're mushrooms," he says, as if I am so far gone I can't even recognize the obvious. "You asked for some?"

"Yes, of course I know they're mushrooms. I just didn't expect to be given raw mushrooms. I thought the cook might make something with them. Soup, or maybe a casserole?" Under my breath I say, "Even just sautéed with a little butter would make them more edible."

"I can take them back to the kitchen and ask—" He turns as if ready to walk away, but then halts, awaiting my response.

"No, no, no." I reach out and take the blue Styrofoam box from him, not wanting to give up all that vitamin D. I'll eat them raw if I have to. "Thank you," I say.

"Not a problem." He stays in the doorway for a moment with his eyes on me. He is around Magdalena's age and probably went to school with her. I have a funny feeling he's about to ask me some uncomfortable questions. I prepare to defend myself, to tell him I'm not ready to talk about what happened with Magdalena, but then he finally speaks up. "Anything else?"

"No," I say.

He retrieves his phone from his pocket, taps his thumbs on it for a few seconds, and then walks out. But I call to him.

"Young man!"

His hand grips the doorframe and he peeks back inside. "What's up?"

I don't say anything right away. We hold eye contact as I give him a second opportunity to ask me a question. But he doesn't. Is it possible he hasn't heard the story?

"What's your name?" I ask.

"Brandon."

"Brandon," I say, "have you seen the Centenarian out in the hall?"

"Who?"

"The Centenarian. The woman who is one hundred and two."

"Why would she be in the hall?"

"She comes to see me now and then."

He narrows his eyes. "How?"

"She comes in a wheelchair."

"I didn't think she could even use a wheelchair."

"She manages."

He leans out of the doorway, then peeks back in. "Nope. She's not out here."

"Good." I say.

"Is she bothering you?" he asks. "'Cause Sister Rosario told us to tell her if anyone bothers you."

"No. She's fine. She's just a bit too chatty sometimes, but she's harmless."

"Okay. Good." He leans further in and says in a lower voice, "And Sister Rosario said not to ask any questions about—you know. So no one's gonna bother you about that."

Now I understand. "I appreciate it," I say.

"The adults think it was your fault, but those of us who went to school with her—we know what she was like. We don't blame you."

"That's kind of you to say," I tell him.

He lifts his chin with a smile, and then disappears.

I lean back on my propped-up pillow and peel away the plastic wrap. Picking off the random specks of dirt with my fingernails, I bite into the spongy mushrooms. The boy's kindness touches me, as does Sister Rosario's. This is the first I've heard that she asked the staff to watch out for me and not to question me. I'm protected here. Sister Rosario has been my safeguard since I was a child and she has not given up on me yet.

I feel a sting behind my eyes, but I've no time for sentimentality. I grab my pen and get back to Susan McIntosh's request.

The first time I read a Susan McIntosh article in *Beyond the Veil* I was mourning my third miscarriage. It was the worst one yet. I lost a baby girl in my seventh month. Her fingers and toes were all there. They let me count before they took her away. I begged them to let me.

One, two, three, four, five. One, two, three, four, five. Her tiny pink hands were flawless. Her pretty little toes already had the beginnings of toenails.

She was almost perfect.

The week after I got home from the hospital in Norwood, Mario walked with me to Dorado's Market. Together, yet separated by our silence, we filled a basket with things we hoped might help get our lives back to normal. Waiting in line to pay, I grabbed a magazine. I came across an article by a new journalist, Susan McIntosh, about a mother who'd lost her six-year-old son. Leaning against the candy display, I got caught up reading it.

In the story, the dead boy appeared to his mother late one night, with his deceased grandmother by his side. He told her he was happy and safe and that his grandmother was taking good care of him. He promised he would stay nearby, and said he would leave pennies for his mother, to remind her he was always around. In the following months, pennies showed up in the house, in the car, on sidewalks, in parking lots, in the dryer—

The checker who had scanned all my groceries interrupted my reading to ask for payment. I set the magazine down and fumbled through my wallet for cash. After paying him, he handed me my receipt along with my change—a penny. Just one penny.

Standing there, looking at the little copper coin in my hand, I finally broke. I let out the tears I'd been holding in since they pulled the almost perfect baby from my body.

Mario took me outside by the shopping carts where he held me and let me cry. He said it was all going to be okay, and we could try to have a baby one more time if I wanted to. If I didn't want to go through it again, we could look into adoption. Whatever I needed, he would support me. That was the kind of husband he was. Back in high school, they called him *slow*—not so slow he had to go to the special school in Norwood, but slow enough to only see the good in people and the best in all situations. A real Mr. Brightside. He certainly wasn't an intellectual match for me, but he made up for it with his overabundance of optimism and love. With Mario by my side, I knew I could get through anything, and so that day by the shopping carts, I told him I wanted to try to have a baby of our own one more time.

The penny showing up after I read the article made me believe a miracle could happen. And a miracle almost did happen. I got pregnant again. This one would survive. I could feel it. It was a strong baby that would fight to live.

Five months along, a tractor hit Mario. He worked up in the hills at Saint Therese's Seminary and Vineyard where they produced sacramental wine for Catholic Masses. One of the seminarians, who had never operated a tractor before, was behind the wheel, while Mario stood in front of it, trying to guide him. The seminarian lost control and Mario was hit but thankfully not run over.

I stayed beside him in the hospital, watching him hang on

to life. I couldn't eat. I tried to force myself, but I couldn't get enough in to keep the baby nourished. When the doctors told me Mario would likely remain a vegetable, I tried harder to get food down so at least I'd have this baby in my life. Still, my stomach resisted, burning as if nourishment was torture. The church, Mario's employer, promised they would take care of me financially for the rest of my life, but even that meant nothing to me at the time.

It was a Tuesday when I was taken away from Mario and put in another section of the hospital. In that small room with the stark white walls, they pulled the last dead baby from me. Another girl. I named her Tuesday. I lost her knowing it was my last chance at ever becoming a mother. This grief was the heaviest of all.

I went to the store a week after losing Tuesday and grabbed a copy of *Beyond the Veil* to see if Susan had written another miracle for me. I didn't know where else to look for hope. I needed hope more than I needed food, water, and air. I didn't think I could make it through another day without it.

Again, Susan McIntosh told just the story I needed.

A nine-year-old girl had been in a terrible car accident with her parents and two brothers. Her whole family died, but she survived. She was put in an orphanage and lived there for years. Because of her age, no one wanted to adopt her. The girl was depressed and lonely and wished she had died with her family.

One day an angel appeared to her and told her she had the power to change her life with one simple gesture—a smile. The angel said to put a smile on her face like she really meant it, and the smile would actually convince her insides she was happy. Then her mind and body would begin to feel she was happy. And so the girl began to smile. Every morning when she woke up, she forced one onto her sleepy face, and kept it there as long as her cheeks could stand it.

Doing this had a curious effect. Sometimes she would spontaneously start to laugh, as a smile is but one step away from laughter. The more she laughed, the happier she began to feel. The happier she felt, the more people started to like her. The other kids at the orphanage, who had previously ignored her, now wanted to be her friend. And best of all, couples who came in looking for a child now took interest in her. One couple, who had come in looking for a younger child, claimed they fell in love with the girl's smile and decided to adopt her. Soon, the girl didn't have to force a smile anymore.

There at the grocery store, with tears streaming down my face, I smiled like I'd never believed I could again. My smile stretched so far up my face, I had to squint my eyes. I could actually feel the click in my body's chemistry as hints of happiness bubbled inside of me. Wiping my tears away, I turned my smile toward the people in the market and those I passed on the sidewalk. It was such a powerful smile, some people turned away and some narrowed their eyes. But I held it up anyway, the whole way home, believing it was fixing everything inside of me.

Susan McIntosh saved my life. No matter how sad or lonely I became over the years, I put on my smile, and more often than not, it helped me move on. I wasn't granted the same miracles as the girl in the story, and I was never able to pull anyone into my life through my smile, but it did change me. It showed me I could alter what was happening inside of me even if I had no control over the outside world.

I smile now, remembering that old article and wondering where the girl from the orphanage is today.

The blue Styrofoam container is empty and I am filled with mushrooms. I'm not sure if it's the vitamin D or the smile I am wearing, but I feel energized. There is so much more of my story I have to tell. I might try to stay up all night until I get to Benjamin's appearance—that devastating moment when I realized he was not who I thought he was.

11

The world from my window was small but reliable and familiar. I watched my neighbors come and go. I watched their kids play outside. I watched those same kids grow up and leave the empty-nesters behind. The Petersons across the street, who'd lost three adult kids to the big city, brought a plastic-covered couch onto their tiny porch so they wouldn't be so alone inside. Dixie, two doors down, made fish soup every first Monday of the month to share with neighbors who brought a bowl to her door. Five mouths were now gone from her house—all four children and a restless husband who left town when the kids did. Butch, the widower on the corner, brought Dixie a fresh catch each time he came back from a fishing trip. He also visited her late at night when no one was watching the neighborhood, except me.

I watched my next-door neighbor Frankie California sit in a black Oldsmobile that showed up in front of his house a couple times a month. Sometimes the car took him away for the week, and sometimes he just sat in the passenger seat talking with the driver. The rumors Mario brought home from the winery were usually based on truth, and so I believed the one about Frankie being an ex-mobster from New Jersey now in the witness protection program. What better place to hide than Sam's Town? Frankie showed up at Mass every Sunday, frequented our local stores, kept a small boat down in the bay and fished like the other men in town. He did what everyone else was doing, but he always seemed a little jumpy, a little suspicious. He was the one neighbor who often caught me watching from the window.

Through the framed glass, I witnessed the seasons changing and the houses weathering. The yellow, blue, and green paint jobs all faded to pale imitations of their earlier days. Scattered white and brown discoloration on the walls, like age spots, spoke of the harsh coastal conditions. Both the people and their houses wore their years honestly.

I watched the eucalyptus trees that lined our street thrive to the point of outgrowing the neighborhood. With some, like the tree in front of my house, the surface roots pushed upward, buckling and cracking the sidewalks. There was no stopping the trees from growing into giants even though they'd been planted in a tiny town.

The morning after Magdalena brought the ghost into my kitchen, I sat in my red paisley chair at the window. My anxious hands found refuge inside the rip at the front corner of the cushion. I toyed with the foam stuffing while staring out through the two-inch separation of the drapes. I paid no mind to the people, the houses, or the trees outside. My thoughts kept returning to Magdalena and Benjamin as I tried to make sense of the night before.

That day I stayed at my window until ten, when Charmaine came.

Charmaine Li is the local mail carrier who lives in Norwood. She looks old enough to be retired, yet her bony legs—with loose skin sagging over her knees—move her along as speedily as one of those plastic wind-up toys. She keeps her salt and pepper hair in one long braid, and no matter the weather, she wears a light blue postal shirt with dark blue shorts. An allergy to eucalyptus compels her to wear a white surgical mask over her nose and mouth. Since she never takes it off, the only part of her face I've ever seen is her eyes.

Charmaine parks an old, boxy postal truck over on Dorado. From there, she walks the entire peninsula with her three-wheeled cart, umbrella attached. She's a good worker, focused on her task. No one can complain about mail delivery. It's what she carries with the mail that causes controversy.

To stay on good terms with the neighborhood dogs, Charmaine keeps a baggie of cut-up hot dogs in her pocket. She gives them to barking dogs to quiet them, but she is also known to toss bits to the crows. The unpopular black birds have taken to following her, and on any given day, twenty or thirty might sweep through the neighborhood. The seagulls, pigeons, and hummingbirds flee to the cliffs when the crows come through.

Crows aren't the most well liked birds anywhere, but in Sam's Town they are especially despised. The proper term for a group of crows is a *murder*. That fact is enough to suggest they're bad news, but the crows out here on the peninsula are literally messengers of bad news. In the early days of our town, they seemed to know things they shouldn't be able to know. A murder would swoop in on an area and caw like they were trying to say something, and then there'd be an accident at that exact spot. Sometimes they'd come and hover over a neighborhood like a black blanket, no cawing, but the flapping of all those wings made an eerier sound. That was their signal an earthquake was coming. It never failed. The earth always shook after they'd blanketed a neighborhood. They'd gathered over the cliffs for hours the day before the landslide of 1967.

Understandably, no one in town ever wants to see a crow fly through their neighborhood. And yet Charmaine invites them to follow her. People tried to have her fired years ago but the postmaster in Norwood said she was the only carrier willing to make the drive out here. If we wanted our mail delivered, we had to tolerate her and her crows.

I myself always had a bit of a soft spot for the old crow lady. Of course I didn't like her traveling our neighborhood with such vile company, but I couldn't help appreciating her kindness. Whenever she saw me sitting by the window, she would stop on the sidewalk and sort through envelopes, as if she might have mail for me. I never received any. Saint Therese's Winery paid all my bills after Mario's accident, and I picked up his monthly paycheck at the rest home from the Sisters. I had no family or friends who wrote me. Still, whenever Charmaine showed up on the sidewalk in front of my house, she stopped and double-checked she hadn't missed anything. It was her job to deliver mail, and sometimes I wondered if she felt like she'd failed when she had nothing for me. It wasn't her fault, but I didn't know how to tell her that.

I came up with a plan. I started going to the Norwood post office to mail myself letters and cards with made-up return addresses from fictitious family and friends, altering my handwriting with each one and using envelopes of varying sizes. I found myself writing the loveliest notes, in case an envelope accidentally came open and Charmaine took a peek inside. The letters were quite believable, and though Charmaine never got the chance to read any, she seemed happy to deliver them. In all honesty, I rather enjoyed receiving the letters myself.

The day after Magdalena's visit, when Charmaine showed up on the sidewalk and went through her sorting routine, something unusual happened. The crows gathered in my tree and squawked, as they often did, but this time one separated from the group. He flew down toward my house and swooshed right by my window. I gasped.

Charmaine stopped sorting and watched the crow. It flew back to the tree and then again, swooped by my window. This time, I flinched but held my breath. The third time he did it, I stayed still and watched him.

Up close, the crow was stunning with its thick black wings spread wide. His color pushed so deep into blackness he reflected glimmers of blue and purple. There was something beautiful about this iridescent creature, but I couldn't let myself be distracted. I needed to focus on deciphering his message.

The crows supposedly behaved like this as a kind of warning. But where were the crows before Mario's accident? Where were they when I was about to lose my babies? Why hadn't they come when my mother and father snuck out of town, leaving me without saying goodbye? Or to warn me Benjamin was about to die? They certainly had plenty of opportunities to alert me of coming tragedies.

That's why I didn't believe this crow had come to warn me of anything. He was alone in his rant, the rest of the murder unengaged. This odd bird had something else in mind. Was it a coincidence he showed up the day following the ghost activity in my kitchen? I didn't think so. I had a feeling the bird was tattling on me, letting the neighbors know I was up to no good.

Charmaine watched the crow with curiosity. Then she looked directly at me through the two-inch space between my curtains. While the surgical mask hid her whole face, her narrowed eyes alone told me what she was thinking. I grabbed the edges of the drapes and pulled them together, holding them tightly to disappear from her suspicious stare. I heard Charmaine clap her hands to settle the crow down, and eventually they moved on.

For the rest of the day, I couldn't eat a thing. I'd been caught. Even if it was just a bird, I felt legitimately accused. This could have been the moment that stopped me from committing any further mischief. It *should* have been. I considered telling Magdalena I'd changed my mind. All day, I practiced what I might say to send her away, but when she came to my door that night, I couldn't do it. For goodness' sake, there was a child at my door, and she wanted to come in and spend time with me. Let the crow taunt me. Let our ghost business stain my soul. This night, unlike every other night for the last ten years, I would not be alone.

12

She wore a faded red Coca-Cola T-shirt and white Dolphin shorts despite the cold. Her feet swam in a pair of oversized beige wallabees that looked like they might have once belonged to her grandfather. Her hair was wet, combed straight down to her waist, and smelled like vanilla shampoo. She kept her head down, all her attention on the lemons, at least eight, that she carried in the hollow of her stretched T-shirt.

"I brought more," Magdalena said. "I didn't know how many you still had." Leaning over the kitchen sink, she dropped the lemons into it.

"I have two left in the fridge." I tucked my lips between my teeth to hold back a smile. I had a visitor again!

"Okay, this should last us a while," she said, and that's when I noticed something crawling on her shirt.

"You have a spider," I began to say, and she immediately started screaming, even before actually seeing it. "Shhhh. Someone will hear you," I warned, but she kept screaming and twisting and swatting her hands all over her shirt until I reached over and whacked the spider off. "It's dead," I said, stepping on it to be sure, then grabbing a napkin to wipe the mushy pulp from my bare foot. "See?" I showed her.

"Oh my God," she said as her shoulders collapsed in relief. "I seriously hate spiders. I can't even—"

"Hey, what's going on?" a man's voice called from the backyard. I had to take a moment to register the strange sound. This kind of thing did not happen. Neighbors did not talk to me.

I looked to the girl for guidance. She ducked down, out of view from the window, and motioned for me to go to the door.

Panicked, I made my way outside. Frankie California peeked

over the fence with a flashlight. He shone it right into my eyes without saying a word, like I was some kind of animal.

Squinting at the bright light, I said, "It was just a spider." My voice shook. "I'm sorry. I'm terribly afraid of spiders."

The flashlight stayed on me. "Black widow?" he asked.

"No. No, it was just a garden spider. But it was big."

"Don't need to cry bloody murder. They can't hurt you."

"I'm sorry," I said again, wondering exactly what this ex-mobster knew about bloody murder.

"Sounded like someone was in there with you. You got company?"

"Oh, no-no-no-no." My pitch rose to an unnatural level. "It was just me. I'm alone."

"Sounded like you were talking to someone, though." He held onto his suspicion like a guy who knew a lie when he heard one.

"I was talking—to myself."

He stayed over the fence, just his bald head and piercing eyes visible above the wooden slats. Interrogated by his stare and the bright flashlight, I did my best to look innocent, but with the way he stayed on me, I could tell he had more questions.

"Ever see the wolf spiders they got in Arizona?" he finally asked. It wasn't the question I anticipated.

"No."

"Hmph. You'd have a heart attack if one of them showed up in your kitchen." There was a soft galloping sound, his fingers tapping against the fence. The galloping quickened and my heart beat in synchrony. I had a terrible feeling this was his way of building up to the tough questions. "How about the ones in Florida?" he asked, the flashlight wavering on and off my face. "Ever see one of them banana spiders? Jesus, they look like aliens."

"No," I said again, now realizing this was not an interrogation. It was chitchat—trivial chitchat while Magdalena waited inside for me.

"What about them cane spiders in Hawaii?"

"I've never left Sam's Town," I told him before he went on to quiz me on the spiders in every state.

His galloping fingers stopped. "No kidding?"

"Of course I've been to Norwood," I clarified.

He laughed at that but then steadied the flashlight on my face. "You being serious?"

"Yes," I said, squinting.

"All right. Nothin' wrong with that. Nothin' wrong with finding your place in life on the first try. But don't you ever wonder what else is out there?"

"Well, yes, I wonder," I said. "But I don't require seeing the things I wonder about."

He was silent. I folded my arms.

"I really need to get back inside."

"Yeah. Okay." The flashlight went off.

"Thank you for checking on me," I thought I should say.

"Nothin' to it."

Frankie's footsteps crackled through the leaves all the way to his door and then I heard it close.

I looked up at the night sky—inky black with a spilling of stars. The ocean air lightly salted my tongue, and I could hear the bell buoy still awake. The moment was peaceful and yet my blood rushed through my veins in a hurry. Not a frantic hurry, but more like excitement. I'd avoided getting caught with Magdalena in my house. She wouldn't have to go back home. She could stay with me a little longer.

Magdalena wasn't in the kitchen. She wasn't in the living room either. I was afraid to look in the baby's room—I hadn't opened that door in years. So I looked in my room first.

There she was, on my bed, leaning against a propped-up pillow, holding a whole lemon. I stepped over her wallabees and stood at the foot of the bed, recounting the entire incident with Frankie in as much detail as I could remember. But she quickly lost interest.

"Are you ready to call for Benjamin again?"

"I am."

"Do you have the twenty-five dollars?"

I turned to my old cherry wood vanity and leaned to the left so the crack in the mirror wouldn't distort my image. I smoothed down my hair. Our frameless wedding photo set against the mirror was faded, its edges eaten away by silverfish. I looked into Mario's eyes and silently told him I was sorry before I turned the photo face down.

Opening my sock drawer, I pulled out twenty-five dollars and gave the payment to the girl. Sitting up straight now, she tucked the cash into the waistband of her shorts.

Without a knife, Magdalena bit into the lemon. Juice bled onto her T-shirt and my bedspread. Completely unconcerned with the mess, she squeezed the punctured lemon and waved it so the aroma filled the room. The light began to flicker. A chill filled the air. Benjamin had come again. Magdalena watched him at the foot of the bed with such calm, it was hard to believe this same girl could scream at a little spider.

"Is he saying anything?" I whispered as I carefully sat down on the bed beside her and stared at the empty space where Benjamin stood. The girl ignored my question and stayed focused. Seriousness overtook her as she slipped into the role of a sensitive.

Magdalena dramatically raised an arm toward the door. It slammed shut. She nodded and it opened up again. She pointed to one of my dresser drawers, and it agitated a little before it opened. A pair of my pantyhose crawled over the side, dangling with the toes pointed toward the ground. Magdalena almost smiled as she shook her head and pointed at it again. The pantyhose slid back inside the drawer just before it slammed shut. She looked up and the light above us turned off, and then on, and off again. That was when loud static came from under the bed, followed by music, and then more static. I knew what it was—Mario's transistor radio. In the dark, I reached under the bed and pulled it out. The light turned on and the static transitioned into old ballroom music, a sprightly song featuring a fast-paced accordion. The music played while Magdalena leaned back against the pillow and closed her eyes. I kept my eyes wide, watching for Benjamin.

When the song ended Magdalena opened her eyes and scooted to the edge of the bed.

"Now it's time to send you on your way," she began like the last time. "Benjamin? Be—"

"Wait. Don't let him go yet," I said. Twenty-five dollars for that little circus act, and barely a ten-minute visit with the girl? I couldn't let that happen. "I don't feel like I'm getting a sense of him," I said.

"Well, you saw with your own eyes he's here. *I* didn't open the door or turn on the music."

"I know," I said. "I don't doubt he's here, or that you're communicating with him, but if he came back to me from the dead, I don't think he came to close doors and drawers and play music. I'm sure he has things to say."

"Conversations take a lot of energy." Her eyebrows shot up in defense. "I'm doing this for half my usual price."

"I understand," I said. "But can you at least let him stay a while? He doesn't need to perform or talk. Can he stay a little longer just so I can be with him?"

"And do what?"

"Well, we used to read together," I told her. "I can read a little bit to him."

She focused on the foot of my bed as if consulting Benjamin. "All right. Just for a little, and then I have to go home."

I grabbed one of the library books from the stack on my nightstand and sat against the pillow beside the girl. As I began to read, I could tell this was one of those romance novels with steamy descriptions. I might have been too uncomfortable to continue with Magdalena there, but she dozed off by chapter two. And so I kept reading aloud to my invisible companion.

At two in the morning, I'd made it through more than half of the book. Benjamin was still there. Every time I read a love scene, he flickered the light, and that was what kept me going. He and I had discovered a way to recapture our time together inside a story. I wanted to keep him there all night, but my eyes were terribly heavy. I knew I was about to fall asleep, so I closed the book. When I set it on my nightstand, the light turned off on its own.

"Benjamin?" I whispered. "Be gone." The air warmed again as his presence withdrew.

Yet Magdalena was still there. I knew I should wake her so she could get back home to her grandmother, but I was selfish. I wanted her to stay and prolong this one happy night.

I imagined if one of my own daughters had lived, she might crawl into my bed at night and fall asleep with me. Like Magdalena, she'd be tall, her long arms and legs sprawled out, taking up most of the bed. And I wouldn't mind. I'd tuck my arms close to my sides and stay on the edge if I needed to, just to feel my daughter's warmth beside me and hear her slow rhythmic breathing.

In the deep hours of the morning, it's easy to confuse what's real with what should have been. There in the dark, I began to believe the impossible.

After carefully covering Magdalena with a blanket, I took the tiny open space available to me on the edge of the bed. Keeping my body as narrow as a pencil, I lay on my side, facing Magdalena—feeling her warmth, hearing her breath, and smelling the scent of her damp hair. Every now and then her foot would brush up against my leg and stay there, touching me. This wasn't one of the daydreams or fantasies I'd fabricated over the years of a child coming back to me. The girl beside me was physically real. Throughout the night, I would wake and see her there—really there. It was as if I'd found myself in a better version of my life where things had turned out differently. Or I'd just woken from a very long, very sad dream to discover one of my babies had actually lived.

I could barely sleep for longer than thirty-minute intervals. Surges of happiness woke me over and over again, and I could see the miracle with my own eyes. My daughter was home.

13

In the morning, Magdalena was gone. I grabbed the pillow beside me and pressed it to my nose. It smelled of her vanilla shampoo and still felt a little damp. The extra blanket I'd used to cover her was bunched up at the foot of the bed. The lemon with the bite marks was on the floor, and my bedspread was sticky from its juice. All proof that the events I remembered from the night before were real.

In my waking hours, I wasn't confused about who she was. I was embarrassed with myself. How could a grown woman like me pretend this neighbor girl was my child? It was one thing to lose myself in make-believe places and dreamed-up circumstances. But altering the identity of a real person? My imagination had gone too far.

I went to the rest home and spent extra time with Mario to remind myself who I really was. I was his wife, not Magdalena's mother.

The word restless is too small to capture what I felt that day. It was more like the itch that aggravated my neck now inside of me, crawling all along my bones. Being surrounded by the four walls of Mario's room only made it worse. I had to get out.

Sister Rosario and Sister Mary Margaret helped me lift my husband into a wheelchair, and for the first time in years, I wheeled him outside for a walk that overcast day. I took him to the Northside Park along the cliffs overlooking the bay. This was where the community held wedding receptions and birthday parties, and strolled the path on Sundays after church if the weather permitted. I remembered my mother and me coming to fly kites. I remembered Mario and me in high school hiding behind the trees to kiss.

The Northside Park offered the best view in town when it wasn't draped in fog. Sometimes on clear summer afternoons, the majestic, jagged coastline could be seen for miles and miles and the ocean seemed endless. Boats traveling the calm blue sea left faded white trails behind, like brushstrokes toward the horizon. Sunsets, even plain orange ones, always drew a small crowd to the park, but sometimes the summer skies exploded with reds, oranges, yellows, and purples as the sun sank away. Everyone came outside to witness the intoxicating colors, knowing the rest of the year they'd feed mostly on gray.

The day I wheeled Mario to the park, he and I sat together looking down at the fog. It was especially thick that morning, hiding all the boats. Only the bell buoy's light pierced through the mist now and then. The air was fresh with a hint of seaweed drifting up from the water. I wanted to talk with Mario and make this outing enjoyable for him, but I had nothing to say. Magdalena was the only thing on my mind. It wasn't something I could explain to Mario. It wasn't something I could explain to myself yet. And so I sat quietly on the bench, taking long deep breaths the way my mother's doctor once taught me, while the fog slowly lifted. Eventually the sky and sea blended together in a faded blue, the emptiness so great, so peaceful, I lost myself in it.

The church bell rang out the hour twice during our stay. Few other noises disrupted our quiet until a distinctive, rather evocative sound jolted me back to my senses—the cawing crows.

I turned to see Charmaine rounding the corner down the street, a murder of crows in her wake. While she slipped mail into the metal slots on each door, the black birds glided out toward the cliffs, swooping and soaring, and then circled back toward Charmaine. We were far down the street from her, and yet my heart hammered in my chest. What if the crow that had taunted me at my house came to attack me? In a panicked rush, I maneuvered the wheelchair off the pathway and headed down the block. My quick pace along the uneven sidewalks caused Mario's languid body to slide down in his seat. I had to stop and try to lift him back in place, but it was too difficult to pull him up. I could hear the crows getting closer. With a whispered apology, I sped my slumped husband along while hanging onto the back of his robe, his body bouncing with the rough ride.

Somehow I successfully got him back to the rest home, only to find he'd lost a slipper and his foot had been dragged across the pavement. The Sisters cringed at all the blood but didn't remark on my carelessness. In fact, Sister Rosario insisted the outing had been good for him as she cleaned and bandaged his foot.

There was nothing soft or sweet about Sister Rosario. She could have successfully run an army had she not chosen a religious life. Her compassion was ambitious and rarely came with a smile. When the kids at school teased me, she didn't ask me how I felt. She simply acted—removing me from a situation or swatting the bottoms of my tormentors. Though I didn't understand Spanish, on those occasions I could tell she was fuming at them under her breath. Her verbal tirade on my behalf felt like affection.

Before I left that day, she gave me Mario's paycheck and took hold of my hand. She squeezed it so tight I had to hold my breath. "You gave your husband a good day," she said. "A few little scratches won't bother him. Don't let it bother you."

"I won't," I told her, and yet during my entire walk to the store, I dug my fingernails into my neck since I couldn't reach my itching bones.

14

Dorado's Market never updated their album collection. The turntable at the front of the store played the same music over and over. Big speakers, mounted near the ceiling, kept up a steady stream of Fleetwood Mac, the Carpenters, the Beatles, Joni Mitchell, Simon and Garfunkel, and Bob Dylan. A few other albums were too scratched up to play often, though we occasionally heard them on slow days, when the cashier had time to move the skipping needle. Over the years, I let those voices speak to me as if they were my friends. When you don't have real ones you create them where you can.

Fleetwood Mac's "Landslide" was playing when I walked in following my outing with Mario. It was a somber song in our town. Those of us old enough to remember the landslide firsthand faithfully bowed our heads and made the sign of the cross when the song came on. That day I tapped my forehead, chest, left shoulder then right as I headed in to cash Mario's paycheck and buy food.

The small market had a distinctive smell. Occasionally some red meat would go bad and sour the air, but most of the time a fishy stench greeted shoppers. The local fisherman sold directly to the butcher who cleaned, scaled, and filleted the day's catch right on the counter. The market's signature odor was especially potent that day I walked in, as a heap of dead fish lay on the cutting table while the butcher leaned over the glass counter talking with a woman in black.

"What do you mean you don't know what else you could've done?" It was the same voice I sometimes heard from next door, calling Magdalena in for dinner or talking with someone who'd brought clothes to mend. Buttons. "If you'd wrapped it in plastic first, the blood wouldn't have dripped all over my kitchen floor," she complained. "You've got those plastic bags right there. Why didn't you use one?"

"Like I said, I'm sorry."

"You know what a hassle that is? To have to mop the floor when you've got all your groceries sitting on the counter, and dinner needs to be made?"

"I understand." The butcher exhaled, as if this conversation had been going on a while.

"If you understand so well, young man, then why—"

I had to walk away and get that angry voice out of my ears. She was the scariest woman in town. The poor butcher was getting hollered at for wrapping her meat wrong. If she knew I'd hired her granddaughter to conjure a ghost, there was no telling what she'd do to me.

Of all days, I'd chosen the grocery cart with the squeaky wheels. There was only one and somehow I was stuck with it. As I hurried past the meat department, my speed generated a squeal that made everyone look my way. Everyone including Buttons.

I stopped in produce and parked the cart beside the apple table. Peeking back at the meat counter, I saw Buttons still looking at me. I dropped my head and sorted through the apples, hoping she'd lose interest now that I was quiet, but it wasn't long before the sound of clicking heels on the tile grew closer and closer. With my head still down I saw her round-toed, block-heeled, patent leather shoes stop right beside me. She stood uncomfortably close. Her aggressive perfume enveloped me. I froze, too afraid to move. The clicking against the tiles started up again and I thought she was leaving, but I looked up to find she'd simply moved to the other side of the table, facing me.

Buttons was a cold and aged beauty. Her black dyed hair erased any trace of gray, and her heavy makeup painted a pretty but deeply lined face. She always wore black, like other widows in town, but while they appeared ragged and worn, Buttons always seemed put together.

Her attention unnerved me. I desperately wanted to scratch

my neck but I tried to keep still. When I finally peeked up she was still watching me. She must have found out about Magdalena. Now that she was done unleashing her temper on the butcher, she had come for me.

I deserved it, I told myself. I'd gone too far. Inviting Magdalena over to help me with a ghost was bad enough, but then I let myself pretend she was my daughter. Punishment from Buttons would come just in time to stop me from losing myself in further delusion. I held my breath waiting for the attack.

"Saint Rita," Buttons finally said.

I looked up at her, confused. "What?" I whispered.

"Patron saint of loneliness. She helped me when my husband died. Pray to her. Maybe it'll help." With that, she walked away.

That was it. She'd offered me a saint prescription and moved on. She didn't know about Magdalena and me—yet. It was my loneliness she had noticed and in a rare moment of compassion, she told me where to find hope. Maybe she wasn't purely mean and scary after all. Maybe even someone like Buttons had a little good inside of her. And I began thinking deeper along those lines as I pushed my squeaky cart along the narrow aisles of the market. Maybe someone like me, who'd tried my whole life to stay good, had a touch of bad inside. Just a touch. That's how we were made, each of us some unique combination of good and bad. And if God was the one who made us this way, he would surely understand what I was going through. He put these feelings inside of me. If he made them up in the first place, he had to understand.

This train of thought felt like a small support pillow tucked under my heavy conscience. By the time I'd made it down each aisle, and gathered all the groceries I needed, my neck barely itched and even my bones felt slight relief.

While I waited in line, paging through a new copy of *Beyond the Veil Magazine*, one of the checkers changed the album on the turntable. Bob Dylan's voice through the speakers told me not to think twice, it was all right. I nodded. Mario had survived our outing. I had survived Buttons. It really was all right.

That's how the voices at Dorado's Market were. They always knew when to say the right thing to me.

15

E arly evening, I walked back to the rest home to check on Mario's foot. He was sound asleep, peaceful. Leaning over him, I prayed to God he would heal quickly and not feel any pain from what I'd done to him. On my walk home I said another prayer, this one to Saint Rita.

Back at my house, I opened the front door and found Magdalena sitting on the living room floor in the cramped space behind the orange velvet loveseat. It was just far enough away from the wall for her to fit, her long legs pulled up to her chest and her arms wrapped around them. She held her chin high as she stared at the painting above. That small space, wedged between the wall heater and the bookshelf, was somewhere a dog or a cat might hide, but not a girl.

"How did you get in?" I asked. Her unexpected presence had my heart racing.

"I looked under the mat," Magdalena said, pulling my hidden key from under her plaid uniform skirt. "Is that okay?"

"It's fine," I simply said, though it was more than fine. It was wonderful! I didn't think she could sneak away again so soon. But there she was, visiting me for the third day in a row. "What about your grandmother?" I asked.

"She has bingo tonight. I closed my bedroom door so she'll think I'm asleep when she gets home."

I leaned forward to see what she was fidgeting with on her lap. It was the book I'd read to Benjamin the night before. She'd fallen asleep while I was reading but must have heard enough to be intrigued. I wondered if the love story was appropriate for a girl her age.

"My grandma has novels like this," she said to my questioning eyes. "I read them all the time."

I nodded. "Well, why don't you come to the kitchen and read at the table?"

"But your window doesn't have a cover. That guy next door could see me."

I liked her carefulness. "I can cover it up," I said.

Of all the supplies I found in the garage, duct tape seemed to offer the quickest solution. I pulled and ripped, pulled and ripped, using my teeth when the material didn't sever easily. Strip by strip I covered each glass panel of the louver window. While it darkened my kitchen and masked the view to my backyard, the dull silver strips granted me a lovely vision in its place— Magdalena at my table.

When I was young, every day after school my mother poured me a glass of milk while I did my homework. Even if she was still in her robe, or crying at the window waiting for my father to get home, she always took a moment to get it for me. That was what I decided to do for the girl at my table.

Magdalena drank her milk while I stood at the sink facing her. An extravagance of thick, dark hair spilled over her shoulder covering half of her pretty face as she read. I watched the way she ran her finger across the page, like a child touching the story, feeling the magic of the words. The vision gave me a window into her younger self, and I imagined a kindergarten-aged Magdalena learning to read for the first time. Somehow the image included me. She was on my lap, her tangled hair in a ponytail, her little finger sliding across the page as I chanted the words with her. She smelled like potato chips, and her little bare feet kicked at the chair legs as if keeping rhythm with our voices. It was so vivid, like a memory.

Still staring at the girl, another longed-for memory miraculously surfaced. Little Magdalena sat on the floor with a coloring book. She turned her box of crayons upside down and all the colors spilled out as she giggled and—

"What's wrong?" the real Magdalena asked.

"Nothing," I said, turning to face the covered window over the sink.

"Are you okay that I'm reading? 'Cause I could stop and we could call for Benjamin if—"

"No, it's fine. You can read some more. I'm in no rush."

"Then why were you watching me like that?"

I squeezed my eyes shut. The truth was safely hidden in my mind, yet I was embarrassed, as if she could somehow see what I'd imagined. "I'm sorry. I—I guess I just—I'm not used to having someone here. It's been a long time."

"How long?"

I turned to her. "Maybe ten years?"

Her mouth was slightly open, her eyes wide and still. I gripped my wedding band and twisted it back and forth on my finger as we stared at each other.

"Do you have friends?" she asked.

"Well. My husband was the social one." I tried to smile but I could feel the lines between my eyes deepen, giving me that worried look.

"No?" She offered the real answer. She said it without shame. That made it easier to admit.

"No," I said.

She gave the slightest nod. I gave the slightest shrug. She bowed her head and went back to reading. That was it.

Her nonchalance over my friendlessness, a fact most people considered abnormal, made me wonder if she had any friends herself.

I busied myself around the kitchen, trying to keep my eyes off her so those fabricated memories wouldn't surface anymore. But every time I heard her turn the page, I couldn't help glancing her way. It was hard to ignore even that faint sound when mine had been the only sounds in the house for years. Music, that's what it was to me. And along with music came company, a guest at my table. That should have been enough for a lonely woman like me, but I got greedy. I wanted Magdalena to fill more than the emptiness in my house. I wanted her to fill the emptiness in my past.

I poured too much Ajax in the sink. I scrubbed and scrubbed

as a distraction, but each time I heard a page turn, I looked back over my shoulder and there she was. And I remembered. Somehow I remembered all the years she was mine.

The itching in my neck flared up with unusual urgency. I left Magdalena and went to the bathroom for my medicated cream. Sitting at the edge of the bathtub, I rubbed the cortisone onto my neck and scalp for twenty minutes. The thick glob on my skin did nothing.

The reflection in the mirror was worrisome: pale skin blotched with red patches, and matted hair where my shaking hand scratched. It resembled one of my mother's episodes. I wasn't like her, though. I knew I wasn't like her. The doctors confirmed that my anxiousness as a child was not a symptom of my own mental illness but a consequence of living with my mother's. I was okay, even if the mirror suggested otherwise. Looking at my fingers, where the secret childhood scars had healed so nicely, I told myself I was okay.

Magdalena eventually called to me and asked if I was all right. I told her I was having an allergic reaction to the eucalyptus trees. It sounded plausible, since we all knew about Charmaine's allergies. The girl didn't question it. She simply let me know she was ready to call for Benjamin whenever I was. I told her these reactions sometimes lasted a while. She said that was okay because she still had fifty pages left to read. After that, she said nothing.

I finally gave up scratching. I held my head in my hands and let the itching crawl all over my skin. The physical discomfort was nothing compared to the awful feelings inside. I was pretending my neighbor's granddaughter belonged to me. A little make-believe with this mother-daughter idea wasn't so terrible, but I could feel the fantasy growing and pushing on me from the inside, like a pregnant belly. I was afraid, yet again, it wouldn't end well.

16

It's early morning. That familiar foul smell is in the air—leftover broccoli. I open my eyes and there is just enough light seeping in from the hall to see her at the foot of my bed. The Centenarian. She is in her wheelchair watching me. I scramble to sit up.

"What are you doing here?" I ask.

She reaches up to smooth her uncombed hair, but it sprouts back out. Her bifocals are in her lap. She squints at me. "Keeping an eye on you." Her old voice sounds croaky in the early morning. It's not pleasant—almost as unpleasant as her smell. "Making sure no one disturbs your sleep."

"You don't need to watch me. My goodness. This is getting out of hand now."

"But the town has visitors," she says, wheeling closer to me. "They heard about you." She touches my skin. Her fingers are shockingly cold.

"What do you mean?" I ask, pulling away.

"The Miller twins are telling a new story to their guests. Your story. I'm here to keep out any looky-loos."

"Where did you hear this?"

"Those young nuns get a bit chatty when Sister Rosario is not around. I sit outside their office, and that's where I get caught up on the town gossip." She continues in a softer voice. "The Millers have been walking their guests by your house. Telling them what happened. The neighbors put a stop to it, but now there is concern they'll come here, so they can get a glimpse of you—the lady with the ghost. Of course the older staff here won't let anybody in. But these volunteer kids can't be trusted. It's best if I keep watch during the night."

"I'm not comfortable being watched while I sleep."

"It's Sam's Town." She looks away and the hall light illuminates her profile. "Someone's always watching."

Her answer is as eerie as her dimly lit face. I put on my robe, go to the window, and open the drapes. The fog is thick and milky. I can't see anything or anyone. I stare into it, trying to make out the church across the street, but the whiteness has swallowed up God's house.

"What kind of story are the Millers telling?" I ask.

"The best kind." I turn back to her and she is smiling. "It's about an outcast, a pretty girl, a ghost, and an illicit lover."

She knows more about me than she lets on. I close my eyes. "They don't know what really happened."

"They don't care. It's not the truth that makes people come and pay to stay at their inn. They offer something better than the truth."

My hands are over my face now.

"You have to give this story a proper ending, dear."

I look at the old woman through my fingers. She is hunched, frail, and practically blind, but she is hard to ignore.

"What do you mean? How do I give it a proper ending?"

"When you're strong enough," she says, "the ending will come." She puts her bifocals back on and wheels herself out to the hall, where she continues to keep watch at my door.

I must work faster and keep longer hours. The Miller twins and their false stories cannot sabotage mine. Light on, paper in my lap, I lean against the pillow and get back to work.

When I was a child, Norwood teenagers came into town late at night to roam our neighborhoods in search of ghosts. My mother sprayed them with the hose if they wandered near our house since the Norwood police refused to come out to the peninsula for any ghost-related issues.

Aside from the mischievous teenagers, our only other visitors were travelers who'd lost their way and stumbled into our seaside town. They'd stop for a bite to eat at The Mermaid Café and Michelle Lynne, one of the waitresses, always told them ghost stories, sometimes embellishing to get a better tip. Two customers, Patti and Paulina Miller, all the way from Alaska, were so intrigued with what they'd heard, they moved to Sam's Town. They lived in the house where Samantha, the fisherman's wife for whom the town was named, had died.

The corner house on the second block of Dorado Avenue, just past the row of businesses, had sat empty for years after the old fisherman passed away. Though it was widely believed Samantha finally moved on after his passing, no one was willing to buy the place—until the twins came. They turned it into an inn and over-charged tourists who wanted to stay at a real haunted house. A black binder in the lobby shared detailed information about each of the landslide ghosts so the guests could learn more about the nightly visitors. How did I know this? I'd paged through the binder a few times when I stopped by for a copy of *Beyond the Veil* on those occasions Dorado's Market sold out.

The inn was pretty yet eerie, with its turquoise paint job, white diamond-patterned windows, and a pointy roof. Above the highest window, a white sign with black letters read SAMANTHA'S INN. Parked out front was a pink Cadillac—the Mary Kay kind, which explained how the twins supported themselves when they had no guests.

Locals never accepted the two Alaskans who were making money off the town's first ghost and our tragic landslide, but no one fought to close down their business. The truth was, we had a love-hate relationship with the twins. While we condemned the way they used our stories, the steady stream of tourists did bring some fresh life to this otherwise secluded town. Shops on Dorado appreciated the extra business. The kids in town followed the newcomers and studied them as if they were from another world. The older ladies in the bingo group, who often complained about outsiders, tolerated them because the strangers offered fresh fuel for the town's stagnant gossip, something none of those ladies were willing to give up.

Now that I have the opportunity to think about it, I believe the Millers' business legitimized a truth the townspeople had been asked to suppress: we lived in a ghost town. Father Candido forbade us from interacting with ghosts, and in doing so, he asked us to deny what was real. But when visitors came to the inn, our strangeness felt special instead of flawed. In my experience, that is not a small distinction.

17

We never did contact Benjamin that night after my itching episode. When I finally came out of the bathroom, Magdalena was gone. But the memories were still with me. I was too tired to fight them. I lay in bed letting them soothe me to sleep.

As I dozed, I saw a very young Magdalena crawling on the wooden floor in the bedroom and then walking for the first time on the kitchen linoleum. I heard her crying in the middle of the night and I rushed to her room to find she'd had a nightmare. I sang to her and ran my fingers through her hair over and over to quiet her back to sleep. Somewhere near the edge of a dream I found a memory of her losing her first tooth and the quarter I put under her pillow. I saw Band-Aids, No More Tears shampoo, baby aspirin, and ponytail holders in a basket at Dorado's Market. I pushed a stroller along the pathway at Southside Park and people stopped me to tell me how pretty my daughter was. They knew her by name. They knew me by name. Dottie. No reason to preface it with odd. I was just Dottie, the mother of the prettiest little girl in town.

Morning came and I lay in bed trying to get my head straight. Of course I knew it wasn't normal to pretend this girl, who was practically a stranger, was my child, and to imagine events that had never really happened. I hadn't lost my mind. But those fabricated memories—they did something to me.

In the bathroom, I stared into the mirror, wiping away the dried cortisone cream on my neck and hair from the night before. The lonely woman looking back at me seemed to beg for compassion, not judgment. If she promised to never accept this fantasy as a fact, and to hide it in the safety of her mind, why couldn't she keep it for a while?

Looking into her eyes, I considered the harmlessness of it

all. Sure, it was weird, but it wasn't criminal. What if it was just a story she kept to herself? No one would ever have to know. Couldn't she hang on to this innocent little dream of having a daughter since real life had refused her the chance four times? I didn't have the heart to tell her no.

Quieting my rational mind that day, I let the Magdalena story stay. It gave me the courage to open the door to the baby's room, which I hadn't been able to do in years. The room smelled stale and musty. I lifted the window to air it out. A bright overcast sun shone in, and dust particles danced in the air as they lifted from their decade-long sleep on the untouched crib.

I ran my fingers over the thick film of dust, uncovering the beige wood beneath. The crib was as lovely as the day Mario had brought it home to me. With a simple cleanup, it was in perfect condition for a young mother to use. There had to be someone in the community who would take it. I certainly didn't need it anymore, now that my daughter had grown.

I pulled the crib outside and the small wheels squealed as they bumped down my walkway. It wasn't easy to maneuver by myself along the uneven sidewalks. Halfway down the block, the wheels got stuck in the dirt in front of Georjean's house, and from my periphery, I could see her looking out the window. I usually gave my neighbors every reason to ignore me, but that day, I let them see and hear me.

Behind Dorado's Market was a garage open to the whole community. THE EXCHANGE, it said on the door. TAKE SOMETHING, LEAVE SOMETHING. It was where people got rid of things they no longer needed without having to transport them all the way to Norwood.

One of the Miller twins was inside when I got there. The sisters looked too much alike to tell them apart—each one tall, heavyset with platinum blond hair teased into the shape of a raincloud. Patti was said to be the outgoing one and Paulina was shy. The one in the garage noticed me struggling to steer the crib along the narrow walkway and came to help. I figured it was Patti.

"Isn't it exciting when they graduate from a crib to a bed," she said. Being an outsider, she knew nothing about me. "Boy or girl?" she asked before I had a chance to respond.

I swallowed. "Girl."

She smiled wide and I noticed her pink lipstick smeared over her teeth. "How old?"

I looked back toward the entrance to be sure no one who knew me had walked in. "Actually, she's fifteen. The crib's been in the garage for years. I'm finally cleaning things out today."

"Fifteen." She shook her head and made clicking sounds with her tongue. "Those teenage years can be rough. I hope she's not driving you crazy like my daughter did to me."

"Oh, not at all. She's wonderful," I said, placing my hand over my heart and peeking back at the entrance once more. "She's so wonderful, I wish she could stay fifteen forever."

"You're a lucky mom," she whispered. She reached out and set her hand on my shoulder. "I just hope it doesn't all change when she hits sixteen." She winked at me and then made her way through the clutter to browse on her own.

Sixteen—I only hoped I'd still have her then.

I left the crib beside a vacuum cleaner and looked around at what I might take—dishes, clothes, knickknacks. Nothing appealed to me. Touching the baby's crib one last time as if to say goodbye, I left empty-handed, but for the gift of being mistaken for a mother.

Back home, I sat in the red paisley chair drinking a cup of tea. With the drapes barely opened, I noticed the crows gathering in my tree and I knew Charmaine was nearby. As she came into view with her mail cart, one crow separated from the others and began to rant. He started at the base of the eucalyptus tree, aggressively jabbing at the trunk with his beak. I could hear chipping sounds as he tore bark from it. Charmaine watched him for a moment as if trying to understand him. He flew at my window again. I swear his little black eyes looked right into mine. He knew things. He was out to expose me.

A loud voice came from next door and I opened the drapes

a little further to find Buttons on her front step. With reading glasses set low on her nose, she tucked her chin to her chest to peer over them at Charmaine. A pair of pants hung over the seamstress's arm, and she waved scissors around as she shouted something I couldn't quite make out.

Turning the lever on the side of my window, I opened the louvers and heard, "…if you don't shut that bird up, for crying out loud." Charmaine clapped her hands and briskly walked down the street, tossing pieces of hot dogs along the way. The black birds rose from the tree and Buttons went back inside.

But that one crow remained on a low branch, still watching me, still cawing at me. Buttons would certainly come back outside if he didn't stop.

I ran to the kitchen and broke off a chunk of leftover meatloaf from the fridge and warmed it in my hand as I carried it through the living room. Opening the window a bit more, I dropped the meat outside.

The crow must have smelled it or seen it—I don't know which sense informed his hunger. He flew down from the tree and paced along the cracked sidewalk. The meat had clearly captured his attention. The cautious bird strutted back and forth some time before he finally snatched up my bribe and flew off. It was quiet again outside my window.

In the kitchen, I wiped my dirty hands on a towel. I could add feeding a crow to my recent list of indiscretions.

I mixed up a small glass of baking soda and water to settle the nervous feeling in my stomach. Glass in hand, I went to the baby's room to consider how I might make this space more appropriate for the girl now that she'd grown.

18

Butter was the fourth and last item on my simple grocery list. I could have gotten out of the market in no time had it not been for Arlene and Betty standing together in front of the dairy case, deep in conversation. They were two of the most influential women in town, the trendsetters. When I was ten, my mom took me to the beauty shop and we both got perms because Arlene and Betty had gotten perms.

They weren't the kind of women I felt comfortable approaching and saying, "Excuse me." And I couldn't figure out how to reach around them without making it awkward. So I turned the other way and faced the canned soups while I waited for them to leave.

The Beatles' album was on the turntable. "Blackbird" came on and made me think of the crow I'd fed beneath my window yesterday. The song was too soothing to feel my usual frustration with the aggressive tattler. Instead, standing there staring at soup cans, Paul McCartney's affection toward his black bird made me feel a little toward mine. I decided to give him a name. It didn't take much creativity to come up with four possibilities: John, Paul, George, or Ringo. The first three sounded too human, but the fourth sounded like a fine name for a bird. Ringo. That was what I'd call him.

Still humming the song on my walk home, I opened the back door to find Magdalena in the kitchen. A chill in the room told me Benjamin was there as well.

Magdalena wore a long, shapeless lavender dress with beads and tiny bells hanging from the sleeves. Her hair was piled up on her head with chopsticks holding the thick bun in place. Gold hoops hung from her ears and lavender eye shadow brightened her eyes. She looked like a child playing dress up.

"Hi," she whispered as if we were in church. "Is it okay if we start our session now?"

"Um, yeah." I used my church voice as well. "I guess so." I set the groceries on the counter and folded my arms to the coolness.

"I can't stay very long tonight."

"Is your grandmother expecting you back soon?"

"No, I have another client after this."

I lowered my eyes. There on the linoleum, my old brown shoes faced her bare feet.

This night was not going as planned. I'd gone to the market for ingredients to bake cookies. Baking cookies with a living Magdalena seemed far more pleasurable than watching an invisible man open and close my cupboards. Of course we'd spend some time with Benjamin to make Magdalena feel she'd come over for good reason, but he'd grown into a secondary interest. I still felt something for him, and I was curious to know how he'd died, but now I had this child.

"While you were gone, something happened."

"Oh?" I looked back up at her.

"Benjamin communicated."

I wrapped my folded arms tighter around myself. "What did he say?"

"Well, first, he said don't worry about his death. It was peaceful."

I brought my fingertips to my lips. "How did he die?"

"He didn't tell me. He just said he left in peace."

I nodded. "Then what did he say?"

"Well, that's when you walked in. He was in the middle of trying to tell me something." She lowered her eyes—lavender from her brows to her lashes. "It was something about love." She quickly looked back up and the gold hoops swung from her ears. Her curious eyes stayed on me. "Was he your boyfriend?"

"No." I could feel my whole face tense up. "Of course not."

"Don't worry, I won't tell anyone if he was. I keep everything in these sessions confidential."

"But he wasn't. We were just friends."

"Well." She turned her head and looked at me from the corner of her eyes. "Could it be you didn't know? That he was secretly in love with you?" This from the girl who'd devoured a romance novel in one night. "Benjamin," she called out before I could answer, "did I hear you say love? Were you trying express your love for Dottie?" The kitchen lights slowly dimmed and brightened, dimmed and brightened. The girl tried not to smile. I could tell she was amused by the response.

"I would rather you ask him more about his death," I whispered. "Can you get him back on that topic?"

She lowered her chin and looked directly at me. "If you want me to *guide* the conversation, I'd have to charge you the full fifty. I'm only doing this because he's offering the information. Let's just give him the freedom to say what he wants to say." She lifted her arms up and the little bells on her sleeves quietly jingled. "Benjamin," she called out, "I give you this opportunity to let Dottie know how you feel about her."

The lights began to flicker, on-off-on-off-on-off. They wouldn't stop. The pace kept up as fast as my heartbeat. Rather than flattered by this show of affection, I was embarrassed. I backed up to the counter, shaking my head and waving my arms to make it stop, not realizing what was behind me. I hit a glass of water. It flew off the counter and shattered on the linoleum in front of Magdalena. The barefoot girl stumbled and stepped right on broken glass, crying out in pain. "Okay, okay, that's enough!" She swept her hand through the air. "Benjamin? Be gone!"

The flickering stopped. With the lights solidly on, I could see the girl limping toward the table. Blood smeared my floor. She sat in a chair, pulled up her dress and lifted her foot to inspect the damage.

I knelt down before her with a towel and wiped away the blood. A chunk of glass was wedged into the soft skin at the arch of her foot. I gently pressed at the sides to ease it out, like a splinter, but she squealed and the glass didn't budge. I softly ran my finger over the area to feel for a protrusion. I found a slight edge and grabbed it with my fingernails. I pulled. She screamed. I'd gotten it out, but within seconds, we heard his voice.

"What's going on in there?" It was Frankie California over the fence again.

I hurriedly handed Magdalena the towel. She gathered up her long dress and hobbled to the living room, leaving a trail of blood behind her. As I went to the door, I noticed the red on my shaking hands. This was going to look bad.

"Nothing is going on." I stepped outside and he aimed a flashlight right at my face. I held my hands up to my eyes. The metallic smell of blood was strong. I could almost taste it.

"Who you telling to stop? Someone in there bothering you? 'Cause I can come over there and take care of business, if you know what I mean."

"No need to come over." I waved my hands, but kept them up to shield my eyes. "There's no one here with me."

"Then who are you shouting at like that?"

"I—I was just frustrated. There were silverfish," I said, looking down at my feet. My voice trembled. "You know, those little bugs? The ones that eat paper and clothes and things?"

"Silverfish."

"Yes. They got into my flour." It didn't start out smoothly, but once I latched onto this peculiar lie, I had somewhere to go with the conversation. My voice calmed. "I planned to make cookies—for the Sisters. They take such good care of Mario. I never think to do anything special for them, so I came up with an idea. To make them cookies. But now my flour is contaminated." It was a lie, and yet this made-up story, combined with the real story of my night, made me want to cry. In a quivering voice I said, "I was just yelling for them to go away."

He turned off the flashlight, but he didn't move away from the fence. "Why you got duct tape covering your window?" he asked.

I closed my eyes. Aside from hiding the girl in my kitchen and concealing our ghost activity, why else might I have covered my window like that? "I can't afford curtains," I told him. "And sometimes—sometimes I just don't want to see the gray skies outside."

I waited in the silence for him to speak, but he didn't. It was as if he was waiting for me to say something.

"Thank you for checking on me again," I said softly. "But no one is bothering me. Just the bugs."

The sound of crushing leaves and a closing door told me when he went back inside. He wasn't up for chitchat this time. My shoulders slumped. I'd fooled him twice, but I didn't believe I could get away with it a third time. We had to be more careful.

Back in the house, I found Magdalena behind the orange velvet loveseat in that cramped little spot she liked. Her foot was wrapped up in the kitchen towel and her head tilted back as she looked up at the painting on the wall. I brought a roll of toilet paper, hydrogen peroxide, and bandages and sat on the carpet beside her, cleaning up the cuts. Her eyes, covered in all that lavender, were trusting and serene as she watched me.

"Did it bother you?" she asked. "What Benjamin said?"

"No. It's fine. I'm fine."

"I didn't mean to make you uncomfortable."

"I'm not concerned with Benjamin's—" I had no word for what he'd done. "How about I help you to the couch and you rest your foot a bit before you go home."

"But I have to go now. My other client."

"Oh. That's right." I reached into my pocket and pulled out the twenty-five dollars I owed her.

"Thanks," she said, starting to get up from the floor. "Sorry about all the blood. I can come back tomorrow and—"

A loud knock came on my front door. We both froze. Was it her grandmother looking for her? Or Frankie coming back to check if I was lying?

Magdalena crawled to the kitchen as I made the long, slow walk to the door. I didn't bother asking who it was. It had to be

Buttons or Frankie, but if it was a stranger coming to rob me, that would have been a relief. The blood on the floor and on my clothes was deceptively gruesome, and it was unmistakable evidence the girl had been here. I didn't know how I was going to get out of this one.

I hesitated a moment at the door, giving Magdalena enough time to sneak out the back. When I finally opened it, Frankie was down the sidewalk heading back to his place. I must have taken too long. The breath I'd been holding came out in a rush.

Before closing the door, I caught sight of something on the front mat. The object didn't register right away, being so out of place. It was a fresh bag of flour. I stared at it, my mouth slightly open at the strangeness of it—not the flour itself, but the gesture.

I picked it up and carried it inside. The bag felt like the weight of a small baby. Curved to my arm, I had to close my eyes at the sensation.

I set the bag on the kitchen counter and took in this peculiar new life of mine: duct tape over the window, bloodstains on my floor, and a back door left ajar by the neighbor girl who visited me to conjure a ghost. My life appeared even stranger in my mind where those fabricated memories gave me a daughter. I understood what a precarious situation I'd gotten myself into, and yet I couldn't help but feel a trembling inside. This was living. It might be risky and uncertain and even sinful, but I felt unbelievably alive.

With an old rag and a bucket of hot water, I erased most of the evidence that Magdalena had visited my house, but I couldn't help leaving small reminders of our time together: a smear on the floor under the table, one on the cabinet beneath the sink, and one on the baseboard by the refrigerator. I left a streak on the chair leg and a touch of red on the wall leading to the living room. Yes, it was blood. I was aware how macabre a keepsake it was, yet something wouldn't let me wipe away all of it.

19

The next morning, I kept my visit to the rest home brief. Too distracted by my strange and exhilarating life, I didn't have patience for my unresponsive husband.

Mario was asleep when I got there. I pried his eyes open so he would see I'd stopped by. Slightly shaken, as if pulled from a dream or whatever state of consciousness he spent his time in, he looked at me. "Hello, Mario," I said. "I've come to see you." Once he focused in on me, I let his eyes close again so he could go back to oblivion. He drifted off instantly. I left.

The long, two-lane highway from Norwood ends at the base of the peninsula, and the narrower Dorado Avenue continues on into Sam's Town. The bus is too big for our streets, so it veers off into a dirt clearing where the highway ends, and makes a U-turn.

That morning I sat on the bus bench in the clearing, waiting for the ten o'clock. It was late again. The working people of Sam's Town took the earlier bus, and this later route was for personal errands. Because of that, the ten o'clock could be anywhere from on time to forty-five minutes late.

Killing time had never been a problem for me. I'd killed months, even years, with the kind of grace a tree must have—a grace that waits unwearyingly for almost nothing to happen. But there I was, tapping my foot with the agitation of someone who had reason to care about the time.

A group of teenagers in school uniforms were waiting as well. Norwood High School offered classes Saint Mary's by the Sea High School did not, and it was common to see students at the bus stop. The teens had ventured up the hill behind the bench, somewhere in the trees. I could hear their shuffling and smell their cigarettes. Alone on the bench, I twisted around to see if I could find them, but they were well hidden.

Instead my eyes caught the fake tree that stood like an
intruder in the company of our real ones. It was unnaturally
straight and sprouted freakishly perfect symmetrical branches
to disguise the metal underneath. Ugly and out of place, it was
cause for bizarre speculation. When it was first erected, stories
spread around town that it was an alien communication device
or a secret military antenna. One Sunday after Mass, a man
stood at the podium and explained in detail why the tree was
necessary for cellular phone reception. His explanation seemed
legitimate, but there were still suspicious whispers about it since
the people in our town rarely settled for the dull version of a
story.

Still impatiently tapping my foot, I turned away from the
ugly counterfeit tree and set my sights on the anchored boats in
the cove below. In the early days of Sam's Town, the fishermen
constructed a concrete stairway with a metal railing that hugged
the cliff and angled down toward the water. It was, and still is,
the only way to access the cove from above.

While the fishermen made good use of the stairs during the
daytime, nighttime brought a different kind of traveler. The
stairway gave teenagers access to the secluded strip of beach
down below for late-night drinking and other mischief. When
full moons caused extremely high tides, the ocean could flood
the narrow beach, and on one such night two teens drowned. It
wasn't that the water level rose too high or that waves came and
swept them away. While their friends left, those two decided to
swim out to the boats. Drunk and disoriented, they were unable
to make it back to shore.

Their ghosts remained trapped in the cove. That was what
my mother told me when I was twelve. It was one of those late
nights when she couldn't sleep and so she crawled into my bed.

"Don't you go down there like those teenagers did," she
warned. "It's not safe, especially at night. And I don't only mean
because you might drown."

"Why else isn't it safe?" I asked.

"The ghosts," she whispered. "That cove is where the

youngest ghosts of Sam's Town are trapped. They stay on the beach, watching the bell buoy's flashing light—believing it's the light at the other end of the tunnel calling to them."

"Why don't they just go to it then?" I asked.

"Oh, they do." She seemed satisfied by my question, as if she needed it to get to the best part of her story. "But when they get there and find it's nothing but a manmade buoy, they realize they are no closer to finding their way to heaven. So they go back to the beach, only to be drawn out again and again, like little moths to the light."

"How do you know this?" I asked.

As was often the case, her answer was all wrapped up in mystery. "Do you ever hear the bell clamoring out late at night?" I nodded on the pillow beside her. "Next time, listen closely for the longing in its sound. You'll hear it. It's distinctly different from the daytime ringing. Then you'll understand. Those poor young ghosts are trying so hard to get to heaven."

At twelve, I'd heard enough teasing about my crazy mother not to believe all her stories anymore. But I couldn't completely disbelieve them. They stayed with me as possibilities.

After Mario moved to the rest home, if it was late and I couldn't sleep, I often took the concrete stairs down to the cove in search of my children's ghosts. They had never come to the house. Following the penny incident at the market, I never had another sign from any of the four children I'd lost. Part of me wanted to believe they'd successfully moved on to the other side, but another part of me, the lonely, grieving part, wanted something, anything, that would bring them near even for just a few haunting seconds. A simple flickering light, a door creaking open, an object falling off a table—something to make real what I'd been left to imagine. There were no smiles to remember, no tender moments to recall, only the feeling of each child growing inside of me, and that ancient mother-child bond beginning to blossom into a love that would come up flowerless.

I walked those stairs in the deep darkness of many nights,

armed with only a flashlight and the hope that my mother's story was true, that a clamoring bell buoy might reveal one of the tiny spirits I'd lost. But there were no ghosts down in the cove. Night after night, I found nothing but a cold, lonely beach, where I cried along with the weepy sounds of the water lapping toward me. It became my favorite place to mourn, until one night, while I was knee deep in the bitingly cold Pacific, Frankie California showed up in a dinghy. Someone had dropped him off and sped away. When he caught sight of me, he didn't ask why I was there, and I didn't ask why he was there. He simply took my arm at my elbow and helped me up the concrete steps that hugged the cliff. He held me tightly, as if I might try to fling myself over the railing, and kept his grip the whole walk home.

"Nothin's ever as bad as it seems," he said, leaving me at my door. "Sometimes life'll surprise you with a second chance." This from the man in the witness protection program. But, I'd asked myself, what kind of second chance might come to a woman like me?

Sister Rosario showed up the next day and I knew Frankie had sent her. She offered to escort me to the beach during the day but suggested I not go alone after dark. That was when my nightly trips down to the cove ended.

The bus finally came fifteen minutes late, just in time to pull me from the sad memories that had no business haunting me that day—a day I was on my way to a rather optimistic errand. I stopped tapping my foot and rushed to the bus with an eagerness that made the driver look at me, really look at me for the first time. I nodded a greeting and he nodded back as the group of teenagers came running down from the trees.

20

Magdalena came over that night in a pair of powder-blue corduroy pants, a short flowery top, and no shoes but for the wrap around her right foot. I immediately showed her the beanbag I'd found at Goodwill. I told her how the bus driver kindly let me keep it in the stairwell of the bus to transport it home.

"It's much more comfortable than that spot on the floor by the heater. I thought if you ever want to come over and read a book or something."

"What was in here before?" Magdalena asked, walking around the otherwise empty room, her corduroys swishing softly with every step.

"A crib."

"You had a baby?"

"Almost," I said.

She stared at me for a moment and was perceptive enough not to ask any more about it.

The beanbag was a disappointment. Magdalena had something far more interesting to share. Her new cellular phone. She pulled it out of her pocket and said she'd just gotten it that day.

I asked her, "Doesn't your grandmother have a regular telephone at the house you can use?"

She narrowed her eyes. "These don't just call people. They do all kinds of things. Haven't you ever used one?"

"Never."

"Oh." Her eyebrows shot up. "Let me show you how it works."

Magdalena sat in the beanbag and I knelt beside her as she tried to explain all the things the tiny telephone could do. She claimed it could connect with people all over the world.

The thing was barely larger than a bar of soap. I wondered if the salesman had taken advantage of her, and yet it seemed everyone was carrying them around these days. I figured there must be something to them.

There on the new beanbag in the newly cleaned-out room, Magdalena showed me how she could communicate with people and share pictures and videos and ideas, and how she could find information on everything. The phone was complex and fascinating. I might have eventually understood it, but soon Magdalena lost interest in explaining how it worked and just stared into the rectangular device, hypnotized. It was as if I no longer existed.

I sat down on the floor and watched her for almost an hour. The phone seemed to have some kind of magic. She never looked away from it. I hoped it was simply the novelty that captured her, but I would learn over the next couple weeks how addictive it would become.

"My grandma doesn't know I have this," she said before leaving that night. "Would it be okay if I came here to use it?"

"Certainly," I said. "You're welcome here any time."

She kept her eyes on her phone as she got up from the beanbag and headed to the kitchen. I followed behind her. Before reaching the back door, she briefly looked up. "Oh. I totally forgot about Benjamin. Here, let's—"

"No, it's fine," I said. "We should skip tonight."

She stared as if trying to read me. "You sure?"

"I'm sure."

"It's not because of what happened last time, is it?"

"No. Not at all. It's just getting late and I'm tired."

"Okay," she said relieved, then looked back down at the phone and headed to the door. I closed my eyes and listened to the swish-swish-swish of her corduroys until she was gone.

The following weeks, Magdalena showed up at my house every night with the phone in hand. She let herself in when I wasn't home. I'd find her in that small hidden space on the floor behind the loveseat even after I'd cleaned out a room for her and furnished it with a comfortable beanbag. When I came home, she'd briefly look up to say hello before gluing her eyes back on the device. She barely talked to me those nights—but she came. It was all that mattered to me.

The lemons sat on my counter untouched. Some molded and I had to throw them away. Neither of us mentioned Benjamin during this time. She'd become too consumed with that phone. I'd become too consumed with her.

These were the weeks I would go back to if I could, and relive them over and over. These were the nights that felt wonderfully ordinary. We became like family in the way we shared our quiet time. Every now and then she'd start up a conversation, but the talking didn't last long. I didn't mind. What she didn't say she left open for me to imagine, and that made it easier to lose myself in the fantasy of having a real daughter.

While she dallied on her phone, I did my chores, finished small projects, and cooked for the two of us. I made meatloaf weekly, preparing the beef and filling the kitchen with its warm, hearty smells. I froze small clumps of it in an ice cube tray, so I'd have an offering for Ringo each day. Then I dished up plates for Magdalena and me. We sometimes ate at the table together. Sometimes she stayed behind the loveseat while I ate alone, the house quiet but for her phone's chirps and chimes that carried into the kitchen, my fork hitting the plate, the scooting of my chair on the linoleum. It was like music, the simple sounds of our lives overlapping.

She was only with me at night, though. During the days, while Magdalena was at school, I still visited Mario and went to the market. On Sundays I went to Mass and sat with the Sisters. On weekdays, I sat at my front window and watched for Charmaine and the crows. It seemed I'd successfully trained Ringo. Once Charmaine and the other crows were far enough down the street, he'd come back to my tree alone. I'd drop the defrosted meatloaf out the window and the black bird would fly off with his bribe.

After a couple weeks of this exchange, something curious

happened. Ringo began leaving things for me in the planter beneath my window. The first day, I discovered a string pouch with a child's game of jacks inside. The second day, he brought a beer bottle cap. Next a pink plastic coin purse. Later came a fishing hook, a key, bits of sea glass, a compass, a periwinkle crayon, a bike reflector, a ruby earring, and a child's-size tin box with owls on it. I imagined he found these things in backyards and on boats down in the cove. They were insignificant enough that the owners wouldn't miss them, but they were significant to me. It was strange and wonderful having a gift to look forward to each day, especially since it came from a bird who had to somehow carry it to me. I set each of these gifts in a wicker basket kept beside my door.

I wanted to tell Magdalena about them, but I was afraid to interrupt her trance. The phone's spell kept her coming back to my house every night and I was careful not to disrupt our fragile arrangement. My father used to say we had to walk on eggshells when my mother was on the verge of a breakdown. I became good at it as a child, and now as an adult the skill served me well.

21

One night, Magdalena broke our usual silence with the ambiguous words: "She changed her name."

She was behind the love seat. I sat on the couch holding a book, not reading but watching her.

"Who?" I asked.

"That's why I couldn't find her. She goes by Juliette now. Juliette Bravo. What a name," she said, sort of breathy.

This was conversation. She was finally speaking to me, connecting with me after days of quiet company. I went to her and sat on the carpet beside the rumbling heater. That funky, musty Goodwill smell clung to the pink fur jacket she had on that night—an extravagance she wore over frayed jean shorts and a simple white T-shirt.

"Who is Juliette Bravo?" I asked.

She kept her eyes on the wall as she said, "My mother."

I swallowed. I've never been a jealous person by nature, and yet I was filled with envy when the girl called that stranger, the one who had left her, *mother*. Suddenly I was a mere neighbor again.

Never would I have believed I'd align myself with Buttons, but I did when I asked, "What would your grandmother say if she knew you were looking for your mother?"

"I really don't care."

The heater went off. The silence seemed louder than the rumbling. I lowered my eyes, not knowing what to say.

"She's my mother." The girl finally spoke. "Do you know how hard it is to live without your mother?"

In fact, I did know. I nodded and brought my hand to my scalp, where I gently scratched. Not because it itched yet, but because I knew it would.

"I haven't seen my mother in years," I replied. "She suffers from mental illness. My father found an experimental program in New Mexico that might cure her." I paused to give her an opportunity to respond, but she just stared up at the painting on the wall. "It's controversial," I went on. "Some call it a cult, since the patients can't have contact with anyone outside. My mother did sneak a letter to me once, telling me she thought about me every day. I believe she tried to send another, but my father must have caught her. I'm sure she's fine. If she wasn't, she would have found a way to escape. My mother is like that."

I was merely taking a breath, willing to offer more, but the girl took what I'd given as enough.

"I've been waiting my whole life to meet my mom," she said. She hugged herself, the bulky fur coat filling the lonely embrace. "My grandma doesn't keep any pictures of her. She got rid of everything that had to do with her."

"Everything?"

"Everything but the stories." Magdalena closed her eyes, leaning against the love seat.

I waited for the girl to tell me more, but she was lost behind her closed eyes for longer than a minute.

"Stories about your mother?" I finally asked.

"No." Her eyes were back on the wall. "Bedtime stories. The same ones she told my mom when she was little. Sometimes I made myself stay awake, even if I was really tired, and told my grandma I couldn't sleep, just so she would tell me those stories and take me to the same places she took my mom."

The girl slid away from the love seat and lay down on the floor. Her bent arm, covered in pink fur, became a pillow. She drew swirls on the wall with her finger as she went on. "There was the Ark Man, the Commandment Man, the Whale Man, the Lion Man, and the Crow Man."

Noah, Moses, Jonah, Daniel—it seemed Buttons had taken Biblical stories and turned them into more fanciful tales. Except one. I didn't recognize the last one. "Tell me about the Crow Man."

Still lying there, she smiled. "So there was an island out in the middle of nowhere. And these crows would come to trick the people into being bad. The island people were too simple to defend themselves and so when the crows flew in, hatred, jealousy, lust, greed—or whatever sin my grandma decided on that night—would spread throughout the land." She briefly lifted her head to look up at me. "Each night she came up with a new evil." She lay back down on the pink fur and resumed her swirls on the wall. "But there was one man who knew how to conquer them. They called him the Crow Man," she sort of sang. "He was smart and quick and would sit under a tree, and sprinkle breadcrumbs around. Then he would stay so still and quiet, the crows thought he was a statue. When the birds flew in to eat the bread, the Crow Man would swipe them up with his bare hands and kill them." She reached up and mimicked a quick grabbing motion. "Then he would give the dead birds to the priest, and the priest would burn them and bury the ashes in the ground, and the island would be freed from whatever evil they'd brought."

I wanted to say something nice about her little story, but it was terrible. I thought of the "evil" crow I'd been feeding at my window, and how he kindly returned my gesture with gifts. Her grandmother had them all wrong.

"I know," she said to my silence, "it's a lame story. They were all pretty bad, but I only liked them because they were once my mom's."

"It's not that, it's just—well, there's a crow here in town," I said, "who has been dropping little gifts for me in my planter." She lifted her head. "Like today, he brought me this." I went to the wicker basket and pulled out the pocketknife. Magdalena's mouth opened slightly as I showed her the folded knife. "The crows in your grandma's stories may be evil, but the ones in real life are—"

"He carried this?" she asked, now sitting up. I nodded. "What else has he brought you?"

"Small things, like toys and jewelry, fishing hooks, and

random items he could pick up." I brought the basket to her and she touched each item as if it were magical.

"Why do you think he brings you this stuff?"

"Sometimes," I admitted, "to quiet him, when he's causing a ruckus outside, I feed him."

She smiled at my confession, reached for her phone, and huddled over it, quickly tapping her thumbs.

"Let's see what they say about this," she said, though I didn't quite know who *they* were.

In no time, Magdalena was telling me about crows—how intelligent and clever they are, how they use tools, and how their cawing is in fact a complex language. They have the ability to recognize human faces and have been known to give names to significant people. I couldn't help but wonder if somewhere within Ringo's cawing was a name he'd given me.

With the phone's light illuminating her face, Magdalena found more information about crows—how they mourn and have funerals for their dead, how they bend twigs into hooks so they could reach food in tight spaces, and finally, how they leave gifts for people with whom they've connected. I sensed she thought I was special, being one of those people.

It seemed my crow story was far more intriguing than her mother's. It felt like a small victory, like what we had together was better. But when I remembered how this whole conversation had begun, I felt less compelled to consider myself the victor.

"You didn't tell me how you discovered she changed her name," I said. "So you found her? In the phone?"

She looked up at me, pulled away from the crows by a topic far more captivating. Her mother. "Yeah." She smiled. "I finally found her. She's still in Hollywood."

I cleared my throat. "Will you be sending her a letter?"

"I already did." I would have loved an explanation of how a letter could be sent through the small device in her hand, but she brought it back up to her face, and was gone to me again.

I didn't mind losing her attention to the phone. I only worried I'd lose the girl to that woman she somehow found inside of it.

22

These earplugs do nothing to block out the uproar in the hall. Something has fallen, glass has broken, and the old people are in quite a state. I distinctly hear Natalie Teller chanting, "Oh no," and I believe it is Gigi Flowers crying out for help.

It's a challenge pulling myself back to the present after spending hours in the pages of my story. Writing has a strange effect on my mind. It seems to cast a spell on me and blur all sense of time as I travel into another world—a world that's somehow both inside me, and yet far away. Like the place we go in dreams. Whenever I'm forced to return to real life, I have to close my eyes for a while and breathe deeply to readjust. Today there's no time for that kind of resettling with this sudden commotion outside my door. I am somewhere between worlds, lightheaded and disoriented, as I venture into the hall.

"Watch your step. There's glass," Henry Smith says, reaching out to block me with his hand that's missing three fingers. His nubs rub against my bare arm and the unnatural feel of them makes me shiver. I pull away. Standing with my back against the wall, I take in the scene.

One of the framed Virgin Mary paintings is on the lentil-green floor, glass scattered everywhere. Sister Mary Ann is trying to guide all the old people into the dining room so one of the volunteers can clean up the mess, but they won't leave. The stimulation in this otherwise dull place has them more animated than I've ever seen.

Across the hall, Buck Donenfeld is parked in his wheelchair, his eye patch in his hand instead of where it belongs. I turn toward the crunching sounds to find Gigi maneuvering her walker through the glass, trying to explain how she accidentally bumped into the painting and made it fall. Natalie covers her mouth and shakes her head wildly as several other wheelchairs roll toward the glass. I look for the Centenarian, but she's not here.

The fallen painting features the Madonna in an abalone shell holding a small fishing boat up to her heart. It is especially sacred to our town. Unlike Our Lady of Guadalupe, Lourdes, or Fatima, this image is far more personal, portraying our own story—Our Lady of Sam's Town. I watch and listen as the old people speculate on why it fell. Randomness is not an option. Superstition and serendipity rule around here. An omen? A message? A warning? A sign that the Virgin is coming again? Their memories may not be sharp, but their imaginations have not failed them.

I'm sad to see the lovely image damaged, but I conjure my own serendipitous reason the painting fell precisely at this point in my letter. I was just about to tell Susan McIntosh what I witnessed at the church fountain, but I realize there is still more to say about what Father Candido saw there years before.

The hall grows louder as the speculations get darker—a tidal wave, an earthquake that will pull the peninsula away from the mainland, an atomic bomb. These people, at the cusp of death, are now considering grand exits. Their talk unnerves me.

I slip back into my room, close the door, and push the earplugs in tightly. Pen in hand, I lose myself again in that other place as I recall the great miracle of Sam's Town.

On the morning of November 11, 1967, months after the landslide, the new priest who had come to replace old Father McKenzie walked into the church courtyard and came upon a miracle. The Blessed Virgin Mary appeared before the fountain in her long blue robe and veil. The fog was still thick, as it always was at that time, and yet Father Candido said that just above Mary, the sunshine came through like a spotlight. It shone such overwhelming light, Our Lady's robe turned the iridescent turquoise of an abalone shell. Whenever he tells this story, he squints and shades his eyes with his hand, helping his listeners understand it was no ordinary gray Sam's Town morning.

The Virgin Mary spoke to Father Candido that day, and although he tells a slightly different version of the conversation each time he recalls it, two important facts always come through. One, Mary told the priest the town needed to pray for the trapped souls who died in the landslide to help them move on. And two, she promised a lifelong blessing to every person who stayed faithful to Sam's Town and didn't give in to the temptation to leave.

"Who could walk away from the Holy Mother's promise that she will bless you for life?" Father Candido asked his congregation the following Sunday. The answer was no one. Compelled by her promise, everyone who was about to leave over the influx of landslide ghosts now decided to stay. The new priest had saved our town.

The Vatican did not accept the inconsistencies in Father Candido's story, and the review board decided not to proclaim it an official Marian apparition. Their uncertainty was disappointing, but it didn't deter the townspeople from believing. Instead, it encouraged faith in Father Candido, the way a family sticks together when an outsider disrespects one of its own. Our Lady of Sam's Town was real and true, miraculous and sacred. And with her unofficial status, she was ours and ours alone.

One afternoon, I was stuffing clumps of meatloaf into the ice cube tray while Magdalena, still in her school uniform, sat at the table looking down at something hidden in her lap. It wasn't her phone. The battery was depleted so the phone sat on the counter, recharging.

"Do you think Father Candido made up the Mary story?" she asked.

I cleared my throat. "The Mary story?"

"When he said the Virgin Mary appeared to him."

I had been raised on the story. My mother told it, my teachers told it, and Father Candido always brought it up in his sermons.

It was as factual to me as the story of Columbus discovering America or the sardine fishermen discovering Sam's Town.

"No," I said, facing her and wiping my hands on my apron. "He did *not* make it up."

"But how do you know?" She reached for her glass of milk and just held it.

"How do I know?" I'd never been asked such a question. "I just know." She kept her eyes on me. "Every adult I'd ever trusted told me it was true," I tried to explain. "How else do we learn but by what our parents and teachers tell us?"

Without responding, she took a sip of milk and lowered her eyes back to whatever she had in her lap. Her long cinnamon hair fell forward over her shoulders.

I approached the table and sat down across from her. "Why are you questioning this?"

She took a blue pen from her lap and set it on the table. Then she held up her left arm. There, on the inside of her forearm, was Our Lady of Sam's Town drawn in blue ink.

"I got in trouble today for drawing on myself. Sister Mary Margaret made me wash it off." She twisted her arm to look at the artwork. "I think this second one turned out better, though."

Our Lady as a tattoo verged on sacrilege, and yet I couldn't deny its startling beauty. "It's a wonderful drawing," I said, admiring it. "But why didn't you use paper?"

"We were in church. I didn't have any."

"Why were you drawing in church?"

"I was bored." She pushed her hair away from her face.

"What made you decide to draw Our Lady of Sam's Town?" She shrugged. "I don't know."

"She came through beautifully," I said.

Magdalena nodded. She licked her finger and rubbed out a smudge under Mary's feet. "She's the only reason I live here. If it wasn't for her, I could be living in a normal town having a normal life." She took the pen and filled in a delicate line. "If Father Candido never told that story, everyone would have left.

That's what my grandma told me. She said Mary's appearance was a miracle that saved the town." She set the pen down and looked at me. "But I was thinking—what if it was really Father Candido that saved the town? The ghosts from the landslide were making everyone want to leave. So what if he just made up a reason for the people to stay until he could get a handle on the ghosts?"

Her skepticism unsettled me. I worried this generation questioned so much, they might eventually lose all instinct for the miraculous. Then how would God ever communicate with them?

"You know," I said, "people from out of town doubt we have ghosts, but we know they're here."

"Because we see them. And hear them."

"And Father Candido has seen and heard Mary."

"But no one else saw her. What if he really didn't? What if he made it up?"

The old priest's inability to connect with the young generation was no secret. We all saw the way they covered their mouths and laughed during his sermons, or rolled their eyes when he went on for too long, but now here was Magdalena proposing he was a liar. The disconnect was far worse than I thought.

"There are things you know with your eyes and things you know with your heart," I told her. "Sometimes you have to close your eyes so your heart can see better."

"I don't buy that," she said. "You have to keep your eyes open if you want to see."

Her phone made a pinging noise and she jumped up to get it. I watched her lose herself in its world again.

I went back to filling the meatloaf tray, replaying our conversation over and over in my mind. I replayed it while I cooked, while we ate dinner, and then continued going through every detail of what she'd said while I lay in bed. I couldn't sleep, unnerved by her suggestion. Not that I'd ever believe such nonsense about Father Candido, but she had me thinking about it, and that alone felt like a kind of betrayal. I did all I could to search for a shiny spot in that otherwise dark conversation. Before dosing off, I found it.

I'd read enough Susan McIntosh articles to know things are not always as they seem. When I asked Magdalena why she decided to draw Mary, the girl shrugged and said she didn't know. She had an answer for everything except that one question. Her instinct for the miraculous might have been fading, but mine was strong. Preoccupied by her doubts over Father Candido's miracle, she had missed the very miracle of Mary appearing to her right there on her arm.

23

Decades after the miraculous appearance of the Virgin Mary, there was a second extraordinary sighting at the same fountain.

Like every other Sunday morning, the ten o'clock Mass ended and the congregation exited through the main door. People gathered out front to socialize on the sidewalk. As always, I sat with the Sisters in a side pew and we exited through the door that led to the courtyard. Some sort of event was planned that day, and so the Sisters hurried off to the auditorium while I made my way through the courtyard alone.

There was a slight drizzle. I kept my head down as I walked, but when I reached the fountain, I glanced up and saw a man in a long black robe. Though his hair was now long and fell softly past his shoulders, I recognized him immediately. It was the ghost of Benjamin! I had not been able to see him when he visited my house, but there at the blessed fountain he came through with unbelievable clarity.

My smile verged on tears as I watched the man I hadn't seen since our last day together at the library. He pulled pennies from his robe pocket and tossed them into the fountain, closing his eyes as if making a wish or saying a prayer. I thought of *Beyond the Veil*'s penny article and believed this sighting was his way of telling me he was always around.

"Oh, Benjamin," I called to him, regretting my neglect. I'd let all those lemons mold away, thinking only of the girl. "I'm sorry for ignoring you."

He turned toward me. The way he looked at me, it seemed as if he thought *I* was the ghost. I wish I could say he was simply surprised or in disbelief that I could see him, but in truth, I must admit his expression was that of pure horror. It made no sense.

What made less sense was Father Candido's greeting as he approached the fountain. "Brother Benjamin, how do you like our little church?"

"It's lovely," Benjamin said, keeping his eyes on me. The horror in his expression had turned to something more like pain.

Three details struck me: "Brother" Benjamin, the black robe, and the realization Father Candido could see him too. These three indisputable facts transformed the miracle of Benjamin's ghost into a greater miracle. Benjamin was alive.

It's a strange sensation when the brain absorbs new information that doesn't fit in with the beliefs already there. It's like trying to push another puzzle piece into an already completed puzzle. The sharp edges poked at my brain.

By itself, learning that Benjamin was alive might seem like a wonderful revelation, but given the circumstances, the implications were difficult to digest. It meant Benjamin had left me, mid-story, without saying goodbye. It meant Magdalena had been lying to me about the ghost in my house. And it meant the ghost in my house was not the kindly Benjamin, but a stranger. I'd never wished death upon a person, but at that moment I thought how much simpler life would be if Benjamin had remained dead.

Unsteady and lightheaded, I made my way to the fountain and sat down on its concrete ledge.

Father Candido introduced Benjamin to me as a seminarian in his last year of training. For the next several months, he would be staying in the Perch—the room above the rectory, nicknamed for all the pigeons that gathered on its roof.

"Dottie, here, is an exemplary servant of the Lord," the old priest said. "She has faithfully taken care of her unresponsive husband in our rest home for ten years."

Benjamin reluctantly approached me and offered his hand. I took it. The way his fingers wrapped around mine, I found it hard to breathe. I coughed so he would let go. He dropped my hand.

"I'm sorry." His eyes were on mine far too long in the ensuing silence. "About your husband," he finally added.

Father Candido rambled on about the luncheon that was about to begin, and the casseroles and salads the women had made to welcome Benjamin to our church. He was blind to what was happening between us. He told Benjamin to come join the rest of the congregation and then left. But Benjamin stayed.

It was clear now. I was a married woman. He was a priest in training. The ring he wore was the same kind of religious ring Father Candido wore—one that promised him to God, not a woman. What Benjamin and I had together at the library had been scandalous. He did the right thing by leaving. I should have simply said, "Good to meet you, Brother Benjamin," and walked away, but I could not hold in my anger.

"You deceived me." I looked over my shoulder to be sure no one was in earshot. "A priest does not do those kinds of things to an unsuspecting woman."

"I didn't *do* anything." He was defensive. "I wouldn't—" He quickly looked over his shoulder and then back at me. "Dottie," he whispered, "I just wanted to be near you. To feel you. Nothing more."

I bowed my head so he couldn't see my embarrassment. "And then just suddenly leave? Without a word?"

"Please forgive me," he said. "I left the way I did so you would forget about me."

I looked back up. "It's hard to forget someone who simply disappears. I thought of you every single day. I worried about what happened to you."

"I should have left a note. I should have explained. I didn't mean for you to worry."

I closed my eyes. "Please explain now."

"I don't have time."

"Give me something!" I whispered loudly.

He cleared his throat, and that was when I opened my eyes again. "I had to give you up. I'd made the decision to dedicate my life to God and resist the urges that had controlled me for far too long. You weren't my usual type," he said gently. "I thought there'd be no temptation. I thought I could have a woman as a friend. Just a friend." He brought his hands together in prayer, below his lips, and gave that charming smile. "But spending time with you, Dottie, you ended up being the loveliest woman of all."

He tried to take my hand, but I backed away. I swung my arm, gesturing for him to leave and he did. He left me at the fountain and joined the people of Sam's Town. I stayed there, staring at the pennies underwater as the light drizzle blurred the surface.

You ended up being the loveliest woman of all.

Those words lit a fire in me. I dipped my hand into the cool fountain and patted my cheeks to soothe the heat. Then I knelt down and brought handfuls of water up to my face. I'd lost all sense of proper etiquette as I began to splash it onto my skin. It was instinctual. I knew I shouldn't engage in gossip-worthy behavior out in public, but the fire had to be put out.

I heard a chorus of clicking heels and looked up to find a group of women walking through the courtyard. They weren't ignoring me like they usually did. They were staring and their mouths were twisted up in horrible expressions, as if a sloth had emerged from the fountain. That was how I felt—sloth-ish, all wet and drippy, my long body hunched over the edge. With my inappropriate behavior, I forfeited my invisibility. This was the day they would start talking about me again.

24

S he was there when I got home, sitting cross-legged behind the loveseat, staring into her phone. She wore a puffy rainbow vest and frayed bellbottom jeans with torn knees.

"Benjamin is alive," I said, standing over her, dripping onto my carpet. "I saw him today."

She narrowed her eyes as she looked me over. "What happened to *you?*"

"Never mind me," I said, smoothing my wet hair away from my face. "You've been lying to me." After all I'd done so the girl would stay, there I was, no longer walking on eggshells. I was smashing them.

She pressed her lips tightly, neither confirming nor denying. It wasn't guilt I saw in her eyes. She didn't seem to have the capacity for that. It was more like regret at getting caught.

"Who is the ghost in my house? Who is it that you invited into my home?" I demanded, kneeling beside her.

She shook her head. "You're not in any kind of danger, if that's what you're worried about."

"But who is it? I have a right to know."

Her eyes held mine, but her lips didn't move.

"You lied to me. About who it was, about what he said. I trusted you and opened my home to you and even paid you. Isn't it only fair you tell me who you brought into my house?"

She hesitated. "Cecilia," she finally said. "Her name's Cecilia." What was once just a Simon and Garfunkel song that played at Dorado's Market was now a real woman haunting my house. "She's completely harmless. I've known her since I was little," she admitted, and bit her bottom lip.

"Why would you do this? Why would you bring this woman into my house and—"

"You wanted a ghost." She was unapologetic. "So I gave you one."

"I wanted Benjamin."

"You thought it was him. And it made you feel better thinking he was okay. Was it so wrong of me to try and make you feel better?"

I certainly didn't feel better now. I felt humiliated and disappointed, betrayed and heartbroken.

I got up and went to the red paisley chair. Magdalena stayed behind the loveseat. Outside the drizzle had turned to rain, and the world from my window was windy, wet, and gray.

"She took care of me," Magdalena said. I kept my eyes on the rain falling through the tree. "Cecilia watched out for me. The others sometimes got aggressive. The ghosts Father Candido couldn't get rid of were strong. When they wanted my help they didn't care if they put me in danger. I was too young to understand what was happening and when I asked my grandma about these people I saw, she made me go to Father Candido. I didn't like what he did to try and fix me, so I learned to keep it to myself. But Cecilia was different. She protected me from danger. I knew I could trust her." Magdalena came out from behind the loveseat and approached my chair. "I brought her into your home because I knew I could trust her."

This was the truth. I could tell. She'd opened up to me as I was certain she hadn't opened up to anyone else. Her most trusted companion was a ghost. It couldn't have been easy growing up like that. And what had she meant by her vague comment about Father Candido fixing her? Was it the same thing I'd witnessed him do to my mother?

Now I look back on that moment and wonder how it might have turned out if I'd acted with compassion and told Magdalena I understood. What might have happened had I turned to the girl and hugged her, and assured her that, like Cecilia, she could trust me?

But that wasn't what I did. I felt too betrayed to behave like a real mother.

"I was a fool to believe you," I said. "You manipulated me, looking for a way to make money so you could buy that phone. You didn't come to help me. You came to use me."

Without a word, Magdalena turned her back to me. I watched her walk away in her rainbow vest and her bellbottom jeans that were so long, the frayed edges dragged behind her.

"Wait," I called when I heard the back door open. There were things I could have said to her even then, on her way out, that might have brought her back inside. But I only asked, "How do I get rid of this Cecilia?"

"She won't bother you," she said. "Just don't cut any lemons."

The door shut. The girl was gone and my house was back to the way it had been all that time before I knew her—empty, quiet, and lonely. And yet everything, absolutely everything had changed.

25

Ringo came back every day. He no longer followed Charmaine and the rest of the murder. I'd find him alone in the backyard perched on an electric wire, watching my house. I'd spot him in the eucalyptus tree, looking into the front window. When I walked to the rest home or the market, he followed me, and though he kept his distance, I knew it was him. He rarely cawed anymore since he wasn't in communication with the other crows. It seemed he'd taken on a solitary life, no doubt seduced by my meatloaf.

The gifts kept coming—a whistle, a paperclip, another key, a dart, a dog tag, a tiny glass earring, nuts and bolts and screws. I added all the items to the basket beside the door. I began to wonder if Ringo found all these things out in the open or if he'd snuck into garages and houses. What I marveled at was the effort he had gone through to bring them to me. Once he brought a small plastic cardholder with a Saint Christopher prayer card inside. It would not have been easy to pick up had it been lying flat, but he'd managed. Another day he brought a garage door opener that clipped onto a car window visor. I had to assume he'd made his way through an open car window and somehow slipped it off the visor. That was one gift I wish I could have returned, but I did not know to whom it belonged. I only knew the crow was willing to perform complex feats to acquire things for me, and I found it difficult not to feel some affection for him. Now that Magdalena no longer visited me, Ringo was all I had. Even Cecilia had stopped showing up.

I'd thrown away the remaining lemons. In their place, I set loaves of bread on my counter along with other treats for the bird. I bought slightly molded cashews and expired pastries from the clearance table at Dorado's Market, and gave Ringo handfuls of them throughout the day. He became like a pet. I still fed him meatloaf in the front planter each morning, but since he stayed around most of the day, I felt I should give him more. It wasn't the same as pouring a glass of milk for the girl at my table, and yet it did feel somewhat nurturing. I wondered if a pet might have given me comfort after the miscarriages.

But the miscarriages were different. They were final, and each loss so unbearable, I became extremely ill. While I felt sad over Magdalena's absence, I was not sick or depressed this time. After all, I had sent her away. She hadn't died. She was still around. In fact, I made a point of seeing her every day.

Just before eight o'clock each morning, she walked down the sidewalk to school. With the curtains barely parted, I sat in my chair and watched her. She never looked toward my house. The way she so easily disregarded me, I sometimes wondered if the whole experience had been a dream. But then I noticed a spot of blood on the floor from the night she'd cut her foot. It was my proof our time together had been real.

Late afternoons, I found her in her backyard. I spent hours, at different times of the day, watching for her through a knothole in the fence. I'd sit in a plastic chair, waiting for her, peering through the hole. That was how I learned she made a habit of sitting in the far back corner of her backyard just after six in the evening. Too mesmerized by her cellular phone to notice me, I was able to watch her as long as I wanted. The phone's light illuminated her face and I remembered how it felt to have a daughter for the short time she was mine. I hadn't yet thought things through and consciously forgiven her, but the way I missed her and longed to see her every day, the anger over her lie began to drain out of me.

My anger toward Benjamin diminished too, but in a different way. Sundays at Mass, he sat with the altar boys while Father Candido gave his sermon. Every now and then he glanced at me and smiled in such a sweet, boyish way, it was hard to stay angry at him. But I certainly didn't smile back. It was church. I was a married woman. He was almost a priest. With each smile he gave, I would shake my head as if to say *don't do that*, but it only made him smile wider.

This routine of ours confused young Sister Mary Margaret, who always sat next to me. She thought he was smiling at her. Charming and handsome as he was, innocent and virginal as she was, this perceived attention developed into a little crush. I noticed the young nun started showing up to Mass with a touch of Vasoline on her lips and a strand of blond hair peeking out from her habit. She was very ordinary-looking. The gloss on her lips did nothing except highlight how thin and pale they were. I certainly wasn't threatened by her attempts to get his attention, and yet I didn't like that she was trying. Benjamin was *my* secret, *my* sin. Even if I'd had the willpower to let him go, I didn't want anyone to take my place.

After Mass one day, as the rest of the congregation filed out the front door, the Sisters and I got up to leave through the side door. Sister Mary Margaret leaned toward me and whispered, "Don't you think he looks a little bit like Jesus?"

Of course I knew who she meant, but answering her would have made it obvious I'd been watching him as well. So I asked, "Who?"

"Brother Benjamin. The seminarian."

Sister Rosario leaned over me and reached for Sister Mary Margaret's arm. With a firm grip and stern eyes, she whispered loudly, "He doesn't look a *thing* like him."

The old woman might have been a nun for fifty years, but she was not naïve to these kinds of things. Like a strict mother, she tucked the young nun's hair back into her habit and wiped the gloss off her lips with a handkerchief. My heart beat loudly as I witnessed this. I wondered if Sister Rosario might hear it and look my way, only to realize *I* was the guilty one. I was the one Benjamin smiled at each Sunday.

The last thing I needed was to be at odds with the only women in town who still treated me like a human being. As a means of self-protection, I skipped Mass the next few weeks, claiming the stomach flu, a migraine headache, and terrible cramps. Adding to my list of sinful behaviors, I'd now lied to a nun.

I wish I'd felt the appropriate guilt for all I'd done and all I'd become. I wish I'd re-examined my less-than-virtuous behaviors and gone back to my old self. But Magdalena's visits had spoiled me. Given a taste of companionship after a decade alone, I now craved it. It was as if I'd been wrapped inside the safety of a cocoon all those years alone and then the girl came and tore it open. I couldn't go back inside. The cocoon no longer held me.

The house was too quiet. I yearned for conversation. While Magdalena and her grandmother were at the five o'clock Mass, I took Mario's ladder from the garage once again. With a plastic bag on my arm, I climbed up to their tree and picked lemons.

Once the bag was full, I took a moment to look around their backyard from my view above the fence. Off in the back corner, where Magdalena usually sat, I noticed a purple sweater on the ground. She must have dropped it while leaving that lonely spot of hers. On the step, just outside the back door, I saw a cardboard box with twelve slots holding empty wine bottles. I looked from the sweater to the box and back to the sweater. The story those two simple items told was enough to break your heart.

On my way down the ladder, I noticed he was there—Ringo, watching me from a wire. I wondered if somehow he knew what I was doing. I wondered if he might start up his ranting and alert the neighborhood that I was up to no good again. I eyed him as I reached the ground, holding the bag behind my back. His head jerked from side to side, looking at me from one eye, and then the other. One, then the other. His focus was relentless.

"All right. All right," I said and went into the house. Setting the bag of lemons in the sink, I dug a spoon into the fresh meatloaf cooling on the counter. I had already fed him a chunk from the freezer that morning, but he would get a second helping that day, so the bird, who was worse than my own conscience, would keep what he'd witnessed a secret.

26

With just a slice, Cecilia came. I didn't even have to squeeze the lemon. She showed up immediately, as if she'd been waiting for the invite.

After learning her name from Magdalena, I went to Samantha's Inn late one night to look her up in the black binder. The old living room had been converted into a lobby furnished with two pink couches, plastic folding chairs set here and there, eerie portraits on the walls, and two card tables—one with books and photo albums of the town's early years, the other with a coffee maker, Styrofoam cups, and a plate of cookies. A desk sat in front of the hallway, and a gaudy burgundy floor lamp stood beside it casting a dull yellow light that flickered now and then.

One of the Miller sisters came to the desk just as I sat on the couch with the binder. Without questioning me she simply whispered, "Enjoy the stories," and then went back to whatever she was doing. I opened it in my lap and flipped through the pages until I saw the heading CECILIA. There were no pictures, just extravagantly loopy handwriting. Cecilia's story took up three pages, front and back. At the top of the page was a note that most of the information had been obtained from anonymous sources, but in a séance with Cecilia herself, she'd confirmed it was all true. Chills ran up my arms and my neck as I began to read.

Cecilia was unmarried and living with her parents while having an affair with Cooper, a married man living in one of the houses on the cliffs. Everyone in Sam's Town knew about their relationship except Cooper's wife.

Cecilia was eighteen years old when the affair began, and they kept it from Cooper's wife for fourteen years. Cecilia wasn't looking to take him away. She liked the freedom of not being a wife and mother. It allowed her to work full time as an artist, sculpting and painting brilliantly colored Virgin Mary garden statues she sold every weekend at the Norwood County swap meet and in several boutiques in nearby cities. No one in Sam's Town wanted a Virgin statue made by an adulteress, but she sold plenty to those unaware of her reputation.

The arrangement worked perfectly for everyone involved until the night Cooper's wife caught the two in bed. Unable to face the community after such a scandal, his wife took the kids and moved far away, leaving Cooper alone in the house on the cliff.

Cooper liked having dinner ready for him when he got home from work. He liked his martini shaken and poured at six when he walked through the door. He liked a clean house and clean laundry. And he liked the warmth of a woman's body in his bed every night. Divorced and alone, he asked Cecilia to marry him. She didn't want to be his wife. She wasn't interested in doing all the things he thought a wife was supposed to do, but she understood that in order to keep the love of her life, she had to bend.

Cooper was a cheating man by nature. Once his mistress became his wife, he needed a new mistress. He found one in Norwood and only came home to Cecilia half the nights of the week. She was used to sharing him and so she never complained. Every night, she made him dinner, poured his martini right at six, and sat at the table, waiting for him to come home. In their yearlong marriage, she spent more time waiting for him than she spent with him.

Eventually the troubled marriage broke her spirit. Cecilia stopped making her statues. She stopped going to the swap meet. She only left the house to buy food, vodka, and cleaning supplies from Dorado's Market. At night, through her open bedroom window, neighbors heard Otis Redding's "Just One More Day" on repeat. The singer's soulful pleading played over and over from her loud stereo speakers, except those nights when Cooper came home. Then they heard laughter and wild lovemaking. Cecilia lived for those nights.

The morning of the landslide, Cecilia was alone in her bed. A full martini was still on the counter when everything she and Cooper had together slid violently down into the ocean. He never came to see the damage. He never made it to his wife's funeral. No one knew what happened to him, but just as Cecilia had waited for him in life, she continued waiting in the afterlife. For over forty years, she couldn't move on. Her ghost remained in Sam's Town, waiting for Cooper to finally come back to her.

I held the binder for a moment, touched by her story. Though I'd gotten upset with Magdalena for bringing this strange ghost into my house, I now understood there was an actual woman behind the paranormal activity—a brokenhearted woman hanging on to her old life the only way she knew how. With this new information she became real to me, and I felt some responsibility. She was in my house. She was my ghost now.

That first night she came back, I stood there with the sliced lemon in my hand, wanting to tell her I knew her story, wanting to tell her Cooper was horrible and she deserved a better ending than she'd gotten, but I couldn't bring myself to say it. If I brought him up, I'd have to be truthful. I didn't have the heart to tell her Cooper wasn't coming back.

Instead, I said, "I'm glad you're here, Cecilia. I think we could be friends." The lights flickered as fast as hummingbird wings and it made me smile.

My television began to spew loud static and I rushed into the living room. Watching the snowy screen with bits of colored scribbles beneath, I wondered what Cecilia was about to show me. Could she somehow reveal her face? Could she communicate with me? As the picture came through, a woman appeared with more clarity than the Zenith had ever shown.

It was not Cecilia but the writer/detective Jessica Fletcher in a rerun of *Murder, She Wrote*. I sat down on the couch and the coldness beside me suggested Cecilia sat with me. My unpredictable television played Jessica's story clearly while I watched captivated. Even the commercials were fabulous—the way the people spoke to me and filled my home with voices and light.

I thought Cecilia had actually fixed my TV that night, but I came to learn it only worked when she was there. And it only worked on her terms. If I turned it on when she was not interested in watching, the static persisted. More often than not, a book would fall to the floor, letting me know she'd rather I read to her.

Sometimes after Cecilia left, I sat on the carpet behind the loveseat where Magdalena used to sit. Curled up in that small space, staring up at the wall heater and the painting, I tried to imagine what had drawn Magdalena to this spot. It was far less comfortable than a chair or the beanbag I'd bought her. When the heater came on, the loud vibrations were unpleasant, but I stayed in that spot for hours, trying to recapture something about the girl. And miraculously, I did. The more time I spent sitting there, the more the girl in the painting began to resemble Magdalena. The painted girl had lighter skin, her hair was not as long and lush as Magdalena's, and her facial features weren't even that similar, but somehow I managed to see a resemblance. It was as if Magdalena's time behind the loveseat left an imprint of her spirit there, and the painted girl in the red dress kept it alive.

27

Monday, following my second absence from Sunday Mass, I walked into Mario's room and found Benjamin in a white robe, sitting on the edge of the bed. He was reading the Bible to my unresponsive husband. Oh, the confusion of that sight—my faithful self and my unfaithful self reflected in the two men before me. I stood in the doorway, reluctant to step inside until Benjamin looked up and gave me that dreamy smile of his. I narrowed my eyes to hide my pleasure, while my heart raced and my insides fluttered like a school girl.

"Join me as I share the Word with your husband," Benjamin said, patting the bed beside him. If nothing else, I was an obedient woman. How could I refuse a man who was almost a priest and armed with a Bible? Too dizzy to comprehend the passage he read, I rested against my husband's limp arm while feeling the vibrations of Benjamin's voice. I breathed in his intoxicating smell.

The Bible reading didn't last long. Benjamin closed the black book and pulled another book out from underneath it. "I also brought something to read to you," he said quietly. On his lap was Stephen King's *The Shining*, the book we had never finished. "It's all I could do to make up for leaving you."

He placed his hand on my thigh, over my housedress, and gripped gently. I didn't push him away. Even with my husband right there, and the door open to the hall, I let his hand stay.

In the following weeks, Benjamin and I went back to being our old selves. We finished *The Shining* and moved on to new books. He seemed to plan his visits when the Sisters were busy with other residents, and if a volunteer came into the room, he discreetly removed his hand from me and replaced our book with the Bible. He was smooth and confident in the way he effortlessly picked up a verse mid-sentence so the volunteer would quickly leave us alone.

As before, we lived through other people's stories. We adopted each novel's mood—he only brought love stories after we finished *The Shining*—and his hand kept me under his spell. Sometimes his fingers traced softly back and forth on my thigh. Sometimes he squeezed me so passionately his grip left a slight bruise on my skin. Sometimes he came close enough to reach up my blouse. The things he did made me feel like a teenager again, my desire too sweltering for a woman my age. Possessed by such physical passion, I gave in to horrid behavior. For God's sake, my husband's eyes opened sometimes, and instead of stopping our foolishness, I reached over and pushed Mario's lids shut. He faded back to oblivion and I went back to my brazen infidelity.

Benjamin was still a mystery to me. He had come back into my life after I thought him dead, but instead of answering my questions, he maintained his mystique and unfailingly kept to the reading. It was as if we were actors, absolved from our actions while we played out the characters' affections. That was the only rationalization I could come up with. Maybe Benjamin needed protection and justification for his inappropriate touching, and books gave him that.

But over time, his touch alone lost its sweetness. I wanted more from him. I wanted to know him and understand his intentions. I wanted him to know and understand me. When I tried to break from our reading and have a conversation, he put his finger up to his lips to hush me. "Let's not ruin this," he'd say.

"But how would we ruin this?" I finally whispered one day. "At the library, we used to talk. It didn't ruin anything then."

"I have to take a final vow of celibacy in a few months. I'm never supposed to touch a woman again." He gripped my hand with both of his. "Can you give me just this?"

I couldn't imagine *this* was okay in the seminarian rulebook, but apparently the final vow was all that mattered to him. Closing my eyes, I nodded and agreed.

My mother used to say there was a big difference between dipping your feet in the devil's water, and swimming in it. I understand that now. It's easy enough to pull your feet out and wipe the water off. But once you are immersed, once you've let the water cover you and seep into your pores and penetrate your very being, there's no wiping it away. It's the difference between trying a sin and becoming the sin.

To distract myself from what I'd become during the day with Benjamin, I invited Cecilia into my home each night. A slice of a lemon was all it took. She kept me company in the kitchen while I cooked and ate my dinner. She didn't seem to disapprove of me tossing nuts and bread to Ringo in the backyard. Granted, she didn't speak, but she could have slammed the door to let me know how she felt. She accepted my absence when I went outside to watch Magdalena through the knothole in the fence. When I came back inside, we simply picked up where we'd left off. I'd finally found someone who needed a friend as much as I did.

Cecilia followed me into the living room after dinner and joined me as I drank my tea. I told my invisible friend stories from the books Benjamin and I read. I never told her they came from novels, but spoke of the scandals as if sharing town gossip. She seemed to like the stories, flickering the lights and moving the drapes over my front window as if they'd been pushed by a light breeze. Then we'd go on to watch TV or read a book. She stayed for as long as I wanted and graciously left when I asked her to go. "Cecilia?" My voice was slightly more timid than the girl's as I mimicked her dismissal. "Be gone."

One night I sat on the couch wrapped in two blankets, the book I'd just finished reading to her on my lap. It was after midnight. The lamplight beside me slowly faded then glowed over and over, like the rhythm of one's breathing.

"I don't know if you still spend time with Magdalena," I said, loud enough to compete with the heater grumbling through the cold. "But if you do still talk with her, can you tell her something for me?"

Earlier in the night, while reading to Cecilia, I felt something between the couch cushions, and when I reached in, I found Magdalena's wooden rosary. I'd never spoken of her since she left, but something about holding those beads in my hand made me want to open up. "Can you tell her I'm sorry?" I asked the ghost. "I shouldn't have been so hard on her for what she did. Of course it was wrong that she lied to me, but I wasn't exactly innocent. It all started because I asked the child to bring back—" I placed my hand over my mouth and shook my head. "I don't know what came over me. I'm not myself these days, doing things I shouldn't be doing," I said through my fingers. "But if you could tell her I'm sorry, maybe I can right one of my wrongs."

The heater went off even though it hadn't finished its work. I took it as a response.

"Thank you," I said. I pulled the blankets tighter over my shoulders and rested my head on the back of the couch. Closing my eyes, and clutching the wooden rosary, I lost myself in memories of my time with Magdalena—real memories. We had those now. I took them with me as I drifted into dreams.

Sometime around two in the morning I woke up shivering. The house was so cold, my hands and feet were almost numb. The lamplight continued its breathing pattern, reminding me I hadn't sent the ghost away. I felt unnerved, as if I'd left the stove on.

"Cecilia?" I whispered. "Be gone." The lamp went off. But only for a moment. It lit back up with a faint glow as if she didn't want to go. "Cecilia?" I spoke louder, the way Magdalena had. "Be gone!" And the light went out.

Though I willingly brought her into my home each night, it would be misleading to give the impression I was one hundred percent comfortable with our time together. Underneath our pleasant friendship was a touch of unease, a slight apprehension that she might turn on me one day. Cecilia the woman was not an aggressive person, but in her condition, stuck between worlds, she wasn't completely herself.

No one in her right mind finds peace in a haunting, but at that point in my life, I needed Cecilia's company. I was more afraid of myself than a ghost.

28

My letter is now a thick stack of papers, and I'm only halfway through the story. I'm worried the completed version will be the size of a Sears catalogue. I don't know what Susan McIntosh will do with it. Will she slice it into smaller sections and create an ongoing series? Or might she turn it into a special-edition issue of *Beyond the Veil*, like when *People Magazine* covers its 100 Most Beautiful People?

"You are detailed, aren't you?" the Centenarian says as she eyes the thick letter in my hands. I didn't hear her come into my room, but now she is beside my bed, in her purple nightgown, hair uncombed. I cover my nose with my hand. Aside from the broccoli smell, I'm pleased to see her. She hasn't come in over a week.

"It's not a simple story," I say.

"No story ever is."

I turn away from her and set the pages on my bed, throwing a pillow over them.

"So protective of it. As if it's your baby." She laughs. It's a crusty old laugh, like the pipes haven't pushed that much air through in a while. It soon turns into a phlegmy cough. Between the broccoli and the mucus, my stomach grows queasy. I have to turn away.

"You never did have a baby, did you?" she says through the congestion. Her words rattle.

"No." How could she know this? I have to assume she's been asking around about me.

"It's a shame," she says. Something is wrong. She isn't her usual friendly self. "Your husband here." She turns her wheels to face him. "He's managed to take care of you even in this most unfortunate condition."

Who could have told her about Mario's paychecks coming every month?

"Yes," I say. "The church supports me. It's very generous of them."

"Generous?" She laughs again, but keeps it light. "You could have gone to the city and gotten a lawyer. No telling how rich you'd be if you sued them."

"I'm not that kind of woman."

"What kind of woman are you, Dottie?" She turns to face me again, and those beady eyes behind her thick glasses stay on me. She wheels closer. "Are you the kind of woman who would call a ghost into her home and trust some wayward girl to manage the situation?"

I cross my arms over my chest. She's becoming mean. It's as if she's possessed. Or maybe someone told her one of the uglier rumors about me and now she despises me like everyone else.

"What do you want from me?" I ask.

With that, she softens her shoulders and gives a subtle head shake. "I want you to toughen up, Dottie," she whispers. "If you can't handle a little harshness from an old woman like me, you're in no position to help Magdalena."

Help Magdalena? She doesn't know what she's talking about. I scoot away from her, up toward the headboard. I lift my arm and try to be discreet as I hit my elbow against the red button.

"How will you do it if you can't even handle me?" she asks, with a wink or a twitch—it's not clear on that wrinkled-up face of hers.

She's not making any sense. I assume old age has her mind mixed up, and while I want to be compassionate, I'm scared of her.

Keeping my eye on the door, hoping a volunteer will show up, I say, "When I'm done with the letter, they will be able to find Magdalena. They will understand what happened to her."

"*They* won't find her, Dottie. *You* will."

She speaks with such confidence, I almost believe her.

29

Cecilia roamed my house. Magdalena sat in the far corner of her backyard looking into her phone, and I sat at the fence watching her through the knothole. That was what six o'clock looked like most evenings, and by seven o'clock, I was back inside for the night. There is no need to repeat details of the days that were all the same. Too many pages of this letter would be wasted on that long repetitive month. In order to move the story forward, I will jump to the day when things changed.

It was almost nine p.m. when I got up from the couch to reheat my tea. Standing by the stove, I heard a noise in the backyard. With duct tape still covering my window, I had to open the door to look outside. A touch of light came from Magdalena's yard, beside the lemon tree. I could hear the leaves rattle.

With the quietest of steps, I made my way to the knothole. Magdalena, wearing that long lavender gypsy dress and chopsticks in her hair, picked lemons using the light from her phone. She placed them into a bag hung from her shoulder. When she'd picked several, she didn't return to her house but went to the gate and exited into the alley. I couldn't imagine where the young girl might be going so late at night. My mothering instinct took over. I couldn't let her go alone. Leaving my back door open, and Cecilia in the house, I followed Magdalena.

In the dark, the distant bell buoy rang out strong and steady. I walked the foggy streets following Magdalena, and kept close to the trees in case she turned around. But she never did. She seemed focused on something ahead.

It was too cold to be outside without a coat. I wrapped my arms around myself as we passed the darkened houses. Dogs barked at us from side yards, but no one bothered to check their windows.

The lemons in Magdalena's bag suggested ghost business. Someone needed her expertise. I was curious to know who else broke the ghost rules like I did. This must have been how the girl continued making money to pay her monthly phone bills and to buy all those frivolous clothes I knew her grandmother would never pay for.

We turned onto Dorado and headed down the residential blocks toward the businesses. Everything was closed except the bar. Its lights were on, and in the quiet I could faintly hear the jukebox playing "Have You Ever Seen the Rain?" Magdalena approached the intersection of Dorado and Dolphin and that was when I knew exactly who had hired her. On the corner was the turquoise house with the pink Cadillac parked out front. The Miller twins. Of course! They made a living promising ghosts to their visitors. Who better to help them than the town's sensitive?

Magdalena went inside and I snuck down the walkway to the side yard. Sitting under a window, I huddled up to keep from freezing while I listened for Magdalena.

"You are welcome to come inside," a voice said from above me. I hadn't even heard footsteps approach. I looked up to find one of the Miller sisters. I felt like a stray dog caught in the trashcans. If I'd had a tail, it would have been tucked between my legs.

Strangely, the heavyset woman smelling of sweet perfume didn't ask why I was there, nor did she accuse me of doing anything wrong. Instead, she held a hand out to help me up. Too scared to do anything else, I took it. Her warmth brought a touch of relief to my freezing hand, but once I was up, I quickly pulled away. She smiled kindly. She didn't seem to recognize me from the day I brought the crib to The Exchange. I assumed this one was Paulina.

"We have the ghost girl in tonight," she said, her hand now on my shoulder, gently guiding me to the front of the inn. "Her sessions are for paying customers only, but you are welcome to sit in the lobby where it's warm, and you can eavesdrop from there." She whispered, "I don't blame you for your curiosity, but we can't allow people to loiter outside. It'll upset the neighbors."

As we approached the pink car, I couldn't contain the urge to ask, "You don't take advantage of the girl, do you?"

"Ha!" she cried out, and put her hand over her mouth. More quietly, she said, "It's the other way around, love. The girl takes advantage of *us*. But what can we do? We need her and so we give her what she asks for."

I nodded, holding my arms around myself, still shivering.

"Why don't you come inside," she tried once again, but I told her I had to go. I walked across the street and around the corner to a yellow house. In the small space between a fence and a bush, I took refuge while I waited for Magdalena. I couldn't let her walk home alone this late. My instinct to protect her was far stronger than my body's need for warmth. I waited almost two hours before I spotted her walking back home. Keeping my distance, I followed until she went through her gate.

My back door had been left open. A rat, a raccoon, or something worse might have crept inside. Already spooked from sitting outside in the dark, afraid of getting caught, I walked inside anticipating something terrible. Instead, I found nothing but an empty house. Even Cecilia was gone.

Wrapped up in blankets, I sat on the floor behind the loveseat. The wall heater rumbled and battled the chilled air I'd let in. It felt like the cold would win, but slowly and steadily, the old heater fought back and eventually warmed my house. I sat there staring at the wall. The painted girl in the red dress now looked even more like Magdalena.

30

Things changed with Benjamin. To be more accurate, I started changing. The intimacy no longer felt mutual. He was taking from me, not sharing something with me. We barely talked. He rarely looked at me. All I got from him was his wandering hand, and it did nothing but dull my passion. I wanted to end whatever it was we were doing together, but he seemed to still need me. It felt wrong refusing him after I'd said yes for so long. What was the proper etiquette when changing one's mind in such matters? I didn't know the answer, and so I continued the visits without protest.

Sometimes old Natalie Teller peeked through the door and started chanting, "Oh no, oh no," at the sight of us together. Benjamin would go to the door and offer her a blessing. It always calmed her. There was no telling what she actually saw, but if she had seen him touching me, who would believe the crazy old lady over the man who was almost a priest? Now and then a high school volunteer came to the door, but Benjamin asked if they would kindly not disturb us while we read scripture. They stopped coming. It seemed he knew how to defuse any situation.

We were on page 113 the morning it finally happened. That much I remember. I was exhausted from the night before. Without a coat, I'd caught a cold waiting outside the inn for Magdalena. My head was too foggy to retain what I'd read and so I reread the page. Benjamin didn't even notice. He was smoothing down my dress, just above my knee. He did this sometimes before reaching underneath. His hand stroked my thigh again and again over my dress, until out of nowhere, another hand appeared. Strong, bony fingers gripped Benjamin's wrist and snatched him away from me.

Sister Rosario. She'd somehow come into the room without making a sound.

The old nun didn't look at me. She kept a firm hold on Benjamin as she walked him out the door. He remained surprisingly calm and convincing as he explained he was comforting me. He told her to ask me and I would confirm it was true. Before leaving, he looked to me with insistent eyes, such eyes I'd never before seen on my passionate friend. *Defend me!* they seemed to say.

I said nothing. Sister Rosario took him away.

Guilt overwhelmed me—guilt for getting caught, and for not defending Benjamin. Then the floodgates opened and guilt over everything I'd done leading up to that moment came rushing through.

I walked home scratching my neck until it bled. What would Father Candido and the Sisters do to me now? It was the first time I realized how much I had to lose. My life, while not an enviable one by any means, was at least a proper life with a home and food and a husband who still managed to provide for me. I wanted desperately to hang on to what I had, and yet I knew I'd gone too far.

I found a set of keys in the planter when I got home. Too preoccupied by the encounter with Sister Rosario, I didn't pay attention to the name on the gold keychain. Mindlessly I took the crow's gift inside and tossed it into the basket.

I didn't want to think about the look on Sister Rosario's face as she pulled Benjamin away from me. I couldn't stand to recall Benjamin's lie—that he was comforting me. I sat at my front window watching the sidewalk in front of Magdalena's house, hoping to catch sight of the girl. If I could just get a glimpse of her, I knew I'd feel better.

Charmaine showed up while I waited. She tripped over the bulging sidewalk in front of my house and caught herself before falling. Standing with her back to me, she eyed the tree and its swollen roots. Her crows cawed from above, but they were lighthearted since Ringo was no longer with them. Charmaine glanced back at me, her eyes showing concern above her white mask. She began to walk toward my window.

A confrontation with Sister Rosario was enough conflict for one day. I couldn't take on the old mail lady too, complaining about the tree. It wasn't my fault it had outgrown the planter. I grabbed the edges of the drapes and held them together, bunching the material to close the gap. My knuckles turned white with my grip and my hand shivered, making the drapes tremble. Charmaine seemed to understand. She left me alone. Still, I held tight, keeping them closed, even as the crows moved so far down the street I couldn't hear them anymore. My grip loosened only when I heard a tap on my window, and a voice—a girl's voice I hadn't heard in weeks.

"Dottie? You okay?"

I released the drapes. There in the small opening was Magdalena. I pushed the drapes wide open and set my forehead and my fingertips up to the glass. A smile came over me and I couldn't get rid of it. I felt no hurt, no anger, no grudge, no judgment. I was too happy to feel those things. Even the guilt and regret from earlier that day no longer ate at me.

"I'm fine, I'm fine," I said, still smiling.

"I saw the drapes shaking and just thought—" She shrugged.

"You know they don't close all the way," I said, "and the mail lady was looking in."

She glanced back toward the street. "The mail lady isn't even out here."

"But she was. Earlier."

"Well, she's gone now. You're safe," she said and looked down at her phone as she turned away.

"But how about you?" I asked loudly. "Are you doing okay?"

She turned back to me. "Yeah. I'm fine." She gave the slightest smile as she scratched her head. Then she brought her little phone back up to her face and walked away.

While we didn't talk things through, I was certain she understood I'd forgiven her. In her own time, she would come back.

31

I was right. That night, after our brief conversation through the window, Magdalena came back. I was on the couch reading to Cecilia when I heard the back door open.

"Hello?"

"Magdalena?" I whispered.

She came into the living room wearing a faded orange sweatshirt with WELCOME TO FABULOUS LAS VEGAS printed in black. Short shorts showed off her long, tan legs, an uncommon sight in our sunless town. She scratched her head as she looked toward the loveseat—not at the painting, but at the empty air. Her eyes latched onto what I couldn't see. She gave a slight nod to Cecilia before turning back to me.

"I need your help."

I stood up. "What's wrong?"

"My head. It's all itchy and I looked up the symptoms. It said I might have lice. Can you check?"

"Did you ask your grandma to look?"

"She's in her room. Watching the Jesus channel." I knew what that meant.

"Well, come on," I said, leading her to the bathroom. I did my best to stay calm and composed as my heart celebrated her return.

Magdalena sat on the edge of the bathtub while I separated her hair to inspect her scalp. Up close, I saw tiny pale dots, like baby raindrops, clinging to single strands of dark hair. Lice eggs were all over her head. It was horribly invasive. I found only a few live, crawling ones, but that was apparently enough to start an infestation.

I took her to the sink and turned on the water. She leaned over and bowed her head so I could remove the tiny eggs and wash them down the drain. My fingernail gripped each nit and slid it down her hair, as if unthreading a needle. Every now and then Magdalena reached up to scratch, but most of the time she kept still and patient. The feel of her hair through my fingers, the smell of her just under my nose, the sight of her vulnerable shoulders slumped so I could reach her, the sound of her slow breathing, and the taste of my tears sliding down to my lips— none of this was fantasy. It was real. And I understood in that moment, with the bright bathroom lights illuminating my hands in her lice-infested hair, if I wanted to hold on to what was real, I would need to accept the best and the worst of Magdalena.

"Is your neck hurting?" I asked after she'd been leaning over the sink for almost twenty minutes. "Do you need a break?"

"No. I'm fine. Are you almost done?" she asked.

I rummaged through her hair to see how much I'd removed. "I got a lot of them. But there's still quite a bit more. You must have had them for a while."

"I probably got them when I watched those kids at church with my grandma. When they had that luncheon for the new guy. Like four weeks ago?"

"A month and a half ago," I said, remembering exactly when they had Benjamin's luncheon.

"Oh God. I've had them that long?"

"Don't worry. We'll get rid of them."

She was quiet. But only for a moment. "Brother Benjamin. Is he *your* Benjamin?"

My hands stopped. "Yes," I admitted.

"Why did you think he was dead?"

I looked up at the mirror. My face was flushed. "I was just— just terribly mistaken."

"Now that he's here, do you ever talk with him?" she asked still facedown in the sink.

I closed my eyes. "He comes to read scripture to my husband." I swallowed hard. "We sometimes talk then."

"Did you tell him anything—about looking for his ghost?"

"No."

"What about Cecilia? Did you tell him about her?" She lifted her head and looked at me in the mirror. "I'm okay sharing her with you, but you can't tell anyone. If Father Candido finds out, he'll send her away. I don't want to lose her."

"I won't say a word about Cecilia."

She let her head fall back toward the sink and I continued picking.

"You're okay with her now?" Magdalena asked.

"She's good company," I told her.

"She is," she said. "I know you were mad. But—I gave you a friend. Didn't I?" It wasn't quite an apology, but it was something, even when I would have taken her back with nothing.

"You did," I said. "Thank you."

32

My devotion to the girl, spending hours pulling tiny eggs from her hair did not solve the lice problem, but it did bring her back into my life. The next night she showed up at my back door with a jar of mayonnaise. She read that slathering mayonnaise into lice-infested hair and leaving it in for thirty minutes a night would eventually smother the creatures and their eggs, and make them all go away. I told her it was worth a try.

Magdalena sat at the kitchen table with her mayonnaise hair up in a towel, looking down at her phone. I poured her a glass of milk, but she stopped me when it was half full.

"I don't drink milk anymore."

"Oh?" I poured the milk back into the carton. "Well, I have some meatloaf here," I said putting on oven mittens and pulling out the fresh batch I'd made for Ringo.

"I don't eat meat anymore either," she said.

I set the loaf on a hot pad and took off the mittens. Turning to face her, I folded my arms. "Why?" I asked.

"I'm vegan now." She spoke as if this small word somehow defined her, as if it could replace all she had been before.

"What is vegan?" I asked.

"It means that I don't eat or use anything that comes from an animal."

"Like a vegetarian?"

"No, they're okay with things like eggs and cheese. Vegans aren't."

I turned to the mayonnaise jar and dug my nail through the ingredients on the label so this new conviction of hers wouldn't sabotage our lice treatments. "What kinds of things can you eat now?" I asked rinsing the balled-up paper from my fingernail into the sink.

"I eat vegetables. Beans, rice, nuts. Grains. Things like that."

"But won't you get sick?" I turned back to her. "You need nutrients from meat and milk."

"People are getting sick *from* the meat and the milk." Her eyes went wide. "It's all the other way around."

"Who told you this?"

"Experts. Doctors. Nutritionists." She held up her phone. "It's all in here."

"People have been eating meat since the beginning of time," I countered. "How can they claim it's bad when it's kept us alive?"

"You can't just blindly hold on to everything you were raised to believe. Just because it kept us alive doesn't mean we can't find healthier ways to eat now that we understand nutrition better. I've spent hours researching veganism and it totally makes sense." She was firm. "I will not eat meat anymore."

I never went through teenage rebellion. My mother couldn't have handled it. Magdalena was a different kind of child, though. She needed rebellion. Growing up without a mother, perhaps she deserved one.

The meatloaf sat on the counter, hot and delicious, but I couldn't eat it in front of the girl. I covered it with foil and set it in the refrigerator.

"I have a can of kidney beans," I said, peering through the cupboard. "And some rice. And some broccoli in the fridge."

"That sounds good."

I thought it sounded terrible, but I cooked it up anyway.

We sat at the table eating while Magdalena went on to tell me about a world she'd discovered on her phone, as foreign as a science fiction novel—poison in our corn, hormones contaminating our meats, superbugs living in our hospitals. She claimed children in Third World countries died while sewing the clothes sold at our discount stores, and pharmaceutical companies were killing people instead of healing them. This was a far cry from her days using the phone to search for her mother. I almost wished her focus was that simple again, but of course I felt relieved she'd moved on from that woman. Juliette must not have replied to her letter. Now Magdalena searched for other tragedies to occupy her mind.

Scooting her chair beside me, she showed me pictures and videos and articles that supported the claims she'd made. The phone was like a television in the palm of her hand. Each new idea somehow connected to more ideas, and the wellspring seemed endless. I could barely follow the visuals, and yet Magdalena touched words and pictures and interacted with this strange portal as if she belonged in it. I understood why the device was so captivating to her, but it was too futuristic and alien for me. I didn't want to learn about that world. I felt safer staying in the one I'd always known.

After dinner I washed the mayonnaise from her hair and she left for the inn, just like every other night. I knew this because I continued to follow her and wait in the bushes so she wouldn't be out in the dark on her own.

But this night was different. It began with the discovery of a large cardboard sign nailed to the eucalyptus tree in front of Georjean's house. The handwritten message read: *Beware! There is a dangerous man in town. If you see anyone suspicious who doesn't belong here, do not approach. Instead, tell Chuck Quinn or William Brown.*

Who was this man? What had he done to be labeled dangerous? I knew our town was prone to exaggeration, and a small story told over and over might grow into a tall tale, but this warning sounded serious.

Secluded from the rest of the world, almost no outsiders ever came to Sam's Town. Our few visitors stayed at Samantha's Inn, and the Miller twins acted like tour guides, rarely leaving guests on their own. We had virtually no crime. But times were changing. Isn't that what Magdalena tried to convey to me with those cell phone stories? Even as we tried our best to stay pure and uncorrupted, we couldn't stop every danger from reaching us.

The cardboard sign made me vigilant. I kept closer to Magdalena when she walked to and from the inn making certain this man could not harm her. Unlike the absent Juliette Bravo, I would keep Magdalena safe.

33

I have one drawer in Mario's room. There is just enough space for the two sets of pajamas, underclothes, and socks they gave me, as well as the clothes I wore when I arrived. Each day when I'm through writing my letter, I hide the pages underneath my clothes.

This morning I open the drawer and spot two silverfish dashing to the bottom. I'm shocked. They're here too! How shoddy that would appear to Susan McIntosh if there were tiny Swiss cheese holes in my letter. She might not read it if it arrived in her mailbox like that.

I inspect the letter for damage and press the red button on the wall.

"Yes, Dottie," a young girl's voice comes through.

"There are bugs in my drawer. Can someone come and get rid of them? Please?"

"I'll send someone to take a look," she says.

I wait, pacing the room. After ten minutes it becomes clear my crisis is low on their list of priorities. I go to the window and push the drapes aside. Clouds filter the sunlight and all vibrant color has drained from the world. I look across the street at the church and the Perch behind it. There must be a hundred pigeons on the roof. It makes me wonder if they were loud and bothered Benjamin while he lived there. I stare at the gray birds, which fit in so well with the entire scene, and as my mind drifts back to uncomfortable memories of Benjamin, there's a knock behind me. I let the curtain fall and go to the door.

Mark, a high school volunteer who walks as slow as a snail and smells like cigarettes, enters my room.

"There." I point to the open drawer. "The bugs are in there."

The boy has no sense of urgency. He takes a moment to pull out the little phone that's buzzing in his pocket and starts tapping away with his thumbs. He seems to have forgotten he is supposed to be working.

"Oh, for goodness' sake," I say.

"Sorry." He stuffs the phone back into his pocket and opens my drawer.

With the tips of his forefinger and thumb, Mark pulls up a pajama top and shakes it over the drawer before setting it on the dresser. He does this with each item, and my dignity is crushed as I watch him shake my panties.

"I don't see anything in here," he says when the drawer is emptied. "They must've crawled out through that gap in the corner."

"Can you repair the gap so they don't get back in?" I'm scratching my neck now.

"I don't actually know how to do that."

"Then bring me some caulking," I say, having learned about home repairs after losing Mario. "I'll do it myself. It just needs some caulk."

He smiles, not even trying to hold back his amusement. Like I'm one of the old people here, too far gone to recognize I'm being made fun of. I pull my shoulders back, as if good posture might show him how young I really am, but he walks out without looking at me again.

Sister Rosario comes to my room. I tell her about the silverfish and she nods her head with the gentle understanding one extends to a child. Without a word, she carefully refolds my clothes and puts them back into the drawer. I watch her. It seems she has not changed in all the time I've known her. Back when I was a child, I thought of her as an old woman who took care of everyone, and she's still that same old woman.

All those years spending lunchtime in her office, I had the opportunity to observe how much Sister Rosario did. When a family was in need, she organized meal trains where the community prepared home-cooked dinners for weeks. She babysat for sick mothers and tutored struggling kids. She visited the elderly who refused to move to the rest home, even the grouchy ones, and ate dinner with them or read to them. She started up collections to help those who couldn't afford to help themselves—when little Olivia broke her glasses in second grade, when old Joseph lost his hearing aid, when Dixie needed a plane ticket to see her dying mother in Minnesota one last time. Sister Rosario even collected money to replace mean Ronnie Nucci Jr.'s front teeth after his pogo stick accident. I donated the two quarters I got from the tooth fairy. Every time he teased me afterward, I looked at those two front teeth and wished I'd never helped pay for them. Unlike me, Sister Rosario didn't regret helping people, even the ones who didn't deserve it. Though always stern, she was the most generous and selfless person I knew. We all called her Sister but she felt more like the mother of our town.

Once my clothes are folded and put away, Sister Rosario closes the drawer and turns to me. "Why don't you shower, get dressed, and come to the dining room for dinner tonight. I'll have someone come back and fix the drawer at that time. It will be good for you to get out of this room."

"I prefer to eat alone," I say.

"But the people here are nice. They're not gossipy like those outside. If you give them a chance, they'll treat you kindly."

I think of the Centenarian. She is obviously privy to gossip the way she knows things about me. And she was not kind the last time we spoke.

"Will the Centenarian be there?" I ask.

She narrows her eyes. "Who?"

"The hundred-and-two-year-old," I clarify.

"No," she says rather quickly. Her response concerns me.

"Is she still alive?"

"She is," she says, watching me curiously, "but very near the end. She's unresponsive."

I am shocked she deteriorated so quickly. While the old woman was a bother, and even aggressive the last time she visited, I am unexpectedly saddened by this news. She was my one friend here. "Will you tell me when she passes?" I ask, my voice soft.

Sister Rosario stares at me for a moment. I can see questions in her eyes, but she lets it be. "I will tell you," she says. She turns away from me and opens my drawer again. She takes out the pants and blouse I wore when I arrived and sets them on the edge of my bed. "I am going to stay for dinner tonight and sit with you in the dining room." She is firm. "I will be back at five, and I expect you to be showered and dressed."

"Yes, Sister," I say.

She leaves the room and I take my pages to the desk where I fall back into my story.

34

We'd gone through several mayonnaise jars. The lice should have been smothered by now, but I told Magdalena we should keep up the treatments to make sure of it. She trusted me.

It was a Tuesday night. The mayonnaise had been rinsed out and I stood behind her, facing the bathroom mirror, her bright yellow sweatshirt more sunshine than I'd seen in a while. I brushed through her tangled, wet hair as she knelt on a plastic step stool. Her phone was in the kitchen beside the outlet, recharging. Without the distraction, she seemed fidgety, searching the clutter on my bathroom counter for something to keep her hands busy.

My tweezers gave her restless fingers something to do. Squeeze after squeeze, the girl created a faint tapping sound, rhythmic like the minutes on a clock. I played along with the sounds she made, brushing in time with her tempo.

Focused on her hair, I hadn't noticed her watching me. When I glance upward, our eyes met in the mirror. Her attention was fierce. Usually she directed it toward her phone. Having it on me made me uncomfortable. I bowed my head and tried to concentrate, but somehow I still felt her stare.

After some time, she stopped tapping. I looked at her again. She took the tweezers to the tip of her finger and pinched the skin. Over and over she grabbed at it as if trying to pull out a splinter. My brushing slowed. I watched her drop the tweezers and rummage again through the clutter on the counter. She picked up my razor. Squeezing it between her thumb and forefinger, she punctured her skin. Her hair was free of tangles, but I kept brushing, watching her as a thin trail of blood ran down her finger. Our eyes met in the mirror, and the way she looked at me, I had a feeling what she'd done wasn't a coincidence. The girl knew.

With her forehead creased up, she asked, "Why did she cut you?"

I held the brush to my chest. "How could you know that?"

Without answering, she put her finger in her mouth to stop the bleeding. Her eyes stayed on me.

"Can you read my mind?" I asked candidly. Too often she seemed to know what I was thinking.

"No," she said. I had a feeling she was lying.

"Then how?"

"The scars on your fingers. I saw them."

"But how did you know she was the one who did it to me?"

"You're not the type to do it to yourself. And you told me your mom was crazy."

That was certainly not the word I'd used, but I nodded all the same.

"So why'd she do it?" she asked again.

I set the brush back to her head and pulled it through her smooth hair, over and over. She let me.

"She cut her own skin first," I explained. "But she didn't do it to hurt herself. She just wanted to witness the miracle of healing." I kept brushing. "She would take her sewing scissors and snip off a bit of skin on her leg, and then she'd spend hours watching it. My father would try to put a Band-Aid on the cut, but my mother always told him no. She would miss the miracle!" I smiled, remembering my mother's delight. "Then she would take a little snippet off my finger to show me that I had the miracle in me too. It wasn't cruel. She was teaching me about the body's power to heal. She wanted me to know I was a miracle." The way the girl looked at me, I could tell she didn't understand. But her rare interest in me, her curiosity over my childhood made me want to go on. "They were small cuts, really small ones that didn't hurt," I explained. "My mother had good intentions. It's just hard to understand if you didn't know her."

"It's weird," she said.

I stopped brushing and folded my arms, not knowing what to say. We just watched each other.

Magdalena set her forearms on the counter and rested her chin on top. "What your mom did was weird, and you don't have to believe it was okay just because she was your mom."

A fifteen-year-old was giving me permission to reopen and re-examine my childhood—yet she was but a child herself. She couldn't understand I'd already digested all that had happened to me. To bring it back up, to regurgitate it would only cause unnecessary grief.

"My mother had good intentions," I said again.

"Father Candido had good intentions when he strapped me to a chair and tried pulling the demons from me." She spoke without expression, without emotion. The facts were powerful enough to make her point. "I was six. My grandma told me to trust him."

"Heavens," I whispered to myself, closing my eyes and remembering my mother's exorcism.

"He didn't get rid of my demons. I didn't have any." She reached down, opened the cupboard under the sink, and pulled out my hair dryer. "He just taught me not to trust anyone more than I trust myself." She plugged it in and then looked at me. She seemed to want to tell me something, maybe something helpful like: *Trust yourself, Dottie.*

I liked that idea. I liked that it would come from a young girl like Magdalena, who had learned the hard way to trust herself. I was grateful she might say something like that, and though that wasn't what she eventually said, I stored the message in my heart as if it had come from her—because in a way, it had.

When she finally spoke, her eyes weren't on me. "I swear, something's just wrong with the people in this town," she said before the loud, agitating sound of the hair dryer ended our conversation.

That night when I followed Magdalena to the inn, I kept my hands in my pockets. For the first time, I was embarrassed by the scars my mother gave me.

35

I hadn't seen Sister Rosario or Benjamin since we'd been caught together. In an effort to avoid them both, I began visiting Mario late each night after I followed Magdalena home from the inn.

The rest home was dark and the Sister on night duty watched television in the dining room. It was easy enough to avoid notice. Mario's eyes were usually open during those late visits. I had a feeling he lived between worlds, and at night, when the spirits awakened, he joined them. There was no telling why he couldn't release from his useless body and move on to the next world. I only knew that while he was still here, I had to remain faithful to visiting him.

I loved Mario in a nostalgic way. It was difficult to feel affection for an empty body, but it was all I had left of the one person in my life who truly loved me. My parents felt some kind of love for me, the kind that comes with shared blood, but as soon as I married, they left town. Still, they'd done what they could for me. My mother's illness was a more pressing matter than staying in town with her adult daughter. I failed to birth them a grandchild anyway. I was grateful they hadn't stayed for the disappointment.

Mario fell in love with me at fourteen. The slow boy and the oddball girl in a relationship made for a lot of teasing. Kids who weren't even bullies couldn't help themselves from dabbling in a little cruelty toward us. It was an ugly time, and yet despite all the tormenting he endured, Mario never left my side. This simple man would not have been my choice for a husband, but I couldn't refuse such a faithful companion, especially when I believed no other man would have me. At nineteen, we married. I did eventually fall in love with him over the years—with his kindness, his generosity, his naïve devotion to a wife who had settled for him. The man was so good, he continued taking care of me after his debilitating accident.

I didn't believe Mario understood what I'd done with Benjamin even though it happened right next to him on his bed. Still, I told him I was sorry. That night, I tried to explain to him how lonely I'd grown over the years and how the emptiness made me weak. I told him how loneliness is a kind of hunger that eats away at the heart the same way absence of food eats away at the stomach. If I'd been without food for too long, it would be justified taking what didn't belong to me in order to stay alive. An apple from someone else's tree, a loaf of bread from the market. I begged him to understand why I took Benjamin. Mario's vacant eyes were incapable of understanding, but at least they didn't judge me. In his unaware state, I had to make all decisions for him. At that moment, I decided he forgave me.

"Then could you understand," I whispered, "why I'd take a child who didn't belong to me?" Again, his lifeless eyes showed no disapproval. I smiled. "She's beautiful. And she's so smart. And she comes to see me every day. She's a miracle, Mario. An absolute miracle."

Gently, I scooted him over on the bed and lay down beside him.

"She's the kind of girl who could change the world." I laughed and put my hand over my mouth. "I don't know why I said that. It's just the first thing that came to mind. I sound like one of those proud moms, don't I, Mario?" I turned my head on the pillow to look at him. His eyes were still open. If he were his old self, he would have said something nice like, *Of anyone in the world, you deserve to be a proud mom, Dottie.* I could just hear him. "You should see the way she dresses. Oh, the colors that have passed through our living room! The child is a rainbow. She's brought more color to my life than I've had in years."

I took his limp hand and laced my fingers through his. I held tight and let myself cry. I hadn't expected to be this emotional, but in the safety of Mario's company, it just came. When I'd cried enough and found my voice again, I told him all about Magdalena.

I felt like I'd gone to confession. My soul was lighter. I thought the feeling might last a while, but stepping into the light of the hall, my smile dropped when I saw who was standing there waiting for me.

"I thought you'd stopped visiting him. I never see you here in the daytime."

"I haven't been sleeping well," I lied. "So I come at night. When I'm awake."

"I didn't think you would neglect your husband."

It had been five days since she'd caught us. I knew I couldn't have avoided her much longer. I bowed my head, ready to receive my punishment.

But it didn't play out as I expected. There in the hall, Sister Rosario took my hand and gently encouraged me to speak up if ever a man tried to take advantage of me again. The old nun seemed to believe I was somehow innocent, that I'd been preyed upon. Had she known I met him weekly at the library for over a year, that I had attempted to contact him when I thought he died, and that I'd freely accepted the arrangement in Mario's room, would she still consider me innocent?

"Sometimes men look for vulnerable women like you," she said, lifting my chin so I could see into her eyes.

"He has not visited since that day," I told her in a weak attempt to defend him.

After a deep inhale, she said, "He asked to leave."

"Leave?"

"That's what men like that do when they get caught."

"Where did he go?"

"Another church not too far from here. I know the Sisters well and I've contacted them. I told them to keep an eye on him." She was quiet for a moment. "I don't know exactly what kind of man he is. What I saw last week was—well. It wasn't right. Dottie, he should not have had his hands on you. Do you understand that?" I nodded, mostly because I understood that was the answer she needed from me. "I don't want to scare you, but I do suggest you stay vigilant. If he comes back to town or contacts you in any way, let us know. If he shows up here in Mario's room, immediately tell someone at the front to call me. And please, Dottie, don't allow him into your home."

I knew Benjamin to be a kind, gentle man, even if he was flawed and sometimes selfish. Sister Rosario's warnings made me wonder if she knew something she wasn't telling me. Had my loneliness blinded me? Had my need for companionship led me to a manipulative man? Fear began to grow where I'd once held deep affection. I started to doubt the Benjamin I thought I knew.

Those cardboard signs, now several of them nailed to trees, brought on a terrible feeling in my stomach. They were put up a day after Benjamin went away. Could he be the dangerous stranger, wearing some kind of disguise to fool the townspeople? Had I lured him back to Sam's Town?

Walking the streets during the following days, I kept looking over my shoulder to be sure Benjamin wasn't trailing me. At night when I followed Magdalena, I kept a close eye out for him. When I returned home and went to sleep, I set chairs up against the front and back doors, and placed a stack of ceramic bowls on top. If he tried to break in, the bowls would fall to the floor and wake me.

Though I knew he was alive, the fear of him unexpectedly appearing made him feel like a ghost again.

36

I was at the back gate heading out to follow Magdalena when Frankie's voice came from his side of the fence. "You hear someone's wandering the peninsula? Someone who doesn't belong here?"

I closed my eyes. "Oh? What has he done?" I asked, scratching my neck there in the dark.

"Tried breaking into Georjean's house. And apparently he's harassing kids too. Can't tell if he's a thief or a kidnapper." Frankie lowered his voice when he said, "Or something else."

The Benjamin I knew wouldn't do these things. But Sister Rosario's version of him might.

"Do they have a description?" I asked, turning to him. Frankie's fingers gripped the top of the fence, his eyes peeking over it.

"Nope. No description. Nobody's seen him except the kids, and they all got a different story. One's got him looking like Santa Claus, one says he's red with horns on his head. You know, they start pulling from their imaginations when they don't got a good answer."

I nodded. In the silence, his fingers drummed the fence with a quick one-two, one-two rhythm. Like a nervous heart. The beat was suggestive, hypnotic. I held my hands to my chest.

"But I was thinking," he finally said, stilling his fingers. "With all that time you spend at your front window, and with these late night walks of yours, I was wondering if you might've seen something."

I didn't realize he'd seen me leaving late at night. What else did he know? "No. I haven't seen anyone," I said.

"If you do see him, come let me know. Any time of night, I don't care. I just want to catch the guy."

"I will," I said.

"You sure you feel safe going out at this hour?"

"I'm fine. I like the fresh air."

"You want me to walk with you? I don't sleep much at night either."

"No," I said. "I prefer to be alone."

"Just be careful," he warned. I nodded and quickly turned away, but then he asked, "You mind me asking where you go?"

Nothing came to me. Not a single lie formed in my mind that might protect me. I feared my silence would affirm my guilt, but Frankie didn't take it that way.

"I understand," he finally said. "We all got our secrets."

He disappeared from the fence, and I left through the gate. My heart still drumming, I rushed to catch up with Magdalena.

I made it to the corner in time to see her enter Samantha's Inn safely. Then I settled into my spot in the bushes and waited.

All night, I couldn't get the children out of my mind. What if Benjamin was watching them like Frankie said? The possibility made me sick. I had to act.

I decided to roam the neighborhoods during the day to keep an eye on the children playing outside. I could never forgive myself if something happened to another mother's child when I knew the predator.

The next morning at eight, I began my patrol of the neighborhoods. I walked each street, watching for Benjamin behind trees and walls, looking down side yards, and going through the alleys. I took streets I hadn't taken in years and checked on every single house, even those with people watching from their windows or their porches. I noticed their suspicious eyes, their whispers, and sometimes their laughs as I passed by, but I held my head high, knowing it was for their own protection. I was already a misunderstood subject of gossip. A little more misunderstanding wouldn't hurt me.

At the very edge of Sam's Town, where the cliffs broke off all those years before, I stood at the chain-link fence. Morning glory crawled all over it. I didn't really think Benjamin would have climbed the fence, but I had to be thorough. Pushing aside the thick layers of those stubborn vines, I tucked my head underneath them and peeked through.

The site of the old broken houses brought me back to my childhood. The scene of the landslide looked smaller through my adult eyes, and while it was still sad, it wasn't scary anymore. I wasn't afraid of the ghosts now. Cecilia gave me a new perspective. In fact, I was curious which house had been hers and Cooper's. I scanned the houses, looking for clues, maybe one of her Virgin Mary statues, but the overgrowth of weeds blanketed all that was left in those front yards. I couldn't tell where Cecilia had lived. Nor could I see any sign of Benjamin.

Untangling myself from the morning glory and letting the stretched and broken vines fall back into place, I moved on to the next street.

At the corner of Minnow and Marlin, at least a hundred pigeons circled overhead and then glided down to roost on the Perch. I was tempted to turn into the courtyard, climb the metal stairs, and peek inside the window to see if Benjamin had gone back to his old room, but if Father Candido happened to be there, I wouldn't know how to explain myself. Instead I turned down the sidewalk toward the front of the church. The door was open. Several women in black dresses and black lace veils came out on the front steps. Rosary hour had apparently just ended, and Buttons and the other widows stood outside the door. They watched me approach with thirsty eyes, as if my presence might offer a sip of gossip. When I reached the steps, I quickened my pace and focused on the other side of the street. There were whispers and a few quiet laughs, but once they were behind me, I disregarded their pettiness and continued on.

I barely made it to the next corner when I heard heels clicking behind me, twice the pace of my own. I turned around. Buttons was trying to catch up to me. The look on her face, the way she tightened her lips and tensed her eyes, it was clear she had something stern to say to me. She knew. Oh God, she finally knew about Magdalena.

I stopped there on the sidewalk, closed my eyes, and bowed

my head as those clicking heels approached. My neck begged for a good scratching, but I was too afraid to move.

Buttons didn't say a word. Instead, I felt her pull at my hair, three quick tugs and then nothing more. Confused, I looked up to see her standing there, a long strand of morning glory in her hand.

"Like throwing them a bone," she said, the skin around her tightened, rose-painted lips all creased up. "They step right out of the Lord's house to find you with weeds hanging from your hair, and they can't resist the jabbering." She tossed the vine into the street.

I patted my hair to feel if anything else was stuck in there. "Thank you," I said in a small voice.

"Gossip is the devil's work. I'll have no part of it," Buttons said, shaking her head and turning away. She seemed angry as she marched back to the church. All the other ladies in black, who'd been watching from the steps, scattered like cockroaches.

For the second time, an encounter with Buttons ended fine. In fact, the mean old lady was an unlikely angel to me in that moment but only because she didn't know the truth about my time with her granddaughter. I felt guilty over her kindness. She had defended me while I secretly betrayed her.

I had a terrible suspicion Magdalena and I could not keep our secret forever. As I continued walking the streets in search of Benjamin, I considered how we might get caught one day. I came up with some troubling scenarios, but my imagination never came close to the disaster I had ahead of me.

37

Day after day, I continued my patrol, looking for signs of Benjamin. Ringo followed me. I was aware of him in nearby trees, watching me as I watched the neighborhoods. I'd stopped making meatloaf for him. Magdalena was offended by meat and I wouldn't risk pushing her away again. I even stopped tossing nuts and bread into the backyard. According to Magdalena's phone, bread was also bad, so I no longer kept any in the house. And when I brought nuts home, Magdalena devoured them. There were never any left over for the crow. In order to please the girl, I had to cut off Ringo.

"My grandma mentioned you yesterday."

"Oh?" I said, turning from the stove. Magdalena's mayonnaise-coated hair was wrapped up in a towel, though a few greasy strands had escaped and fell on her red Charlie's Angels T-shirt. She sat at the table with a jar of peanut butter and a spoon. Without bread, she couldn't make a sandwich.

"She said you had weeds in your hair the other day. And the church ladies made fun of you."

"It was morning glory," I told her. "I didn't know it was stuck in my hair, but your grandmother kindly took it out."

She nodded as her mouth made slow, circular motions with the peanut butter. Once she swallowed it, she said, "She thinks you're sad. She calls you the sad neighbor."

Of course I didn't like hearing that, but something else concerned me more. "Why were you talking about me? Does she know you come here?"

"No. She has no idea." I let my shoulders relax. "She just randomly brought you up and said every time she sees you, you look sad."

"Well." I stirred the lentils on the stove, the smell of onions and garlic rising up. "I feel normal."

"Around here, sad is normal." She set the spoon down and picked up her phone. "I read that places without a lot of sun are the saddest places and have the highest rates of suicide. You don't get enough vitamin D. And that can cause depression."

I'd never heard of a single suicide in Sam's Town. Sometimes the information in that phone didn't apply to us. I wanted to tell her we were different, but I thought it wise to keep that to myself. I could tell Magdalena wanted to be more like those outsiders.

"I can look up other ways to get vitamin D," she said, tapping her thumbs on the phone.

"You know, we used to get it from milk," I dared to say. "It's fortified with vitamin D."

Either she didn't hear me or she chose to ignore me.

I went back to preparing dinner, peeling potatoes and carrots over the sink, the rhythmic sound of the peeler the only noise in the kitchen.

This was my favorite time of the day, cooking and sharing dinner with Magdalena. She and her grandmother had stopped sitting together at the table years ago. Buttons left meals on the stove for her, but Magdalena no longer ate the kind of food the old woman cooked. Lately the girl just threw a helping in the trash to make it look like she'd eaten. It was now my sole responsibility to feed her.

By the time the vegetable skins covered the sink, Magdalena had found an answer. "Mushrooms," she said. "We need to eat mushrooms. If we eat enough of them, we'll get the vitamin D we're missing from the sun."

We. That word stood out to me. *We* need to eat mushrooms. Was I so used to my own sadness, I hadn't even recognized it in her?

"I can get some from the market tomorrow," I told her.

Along with the rice, beans, lentils, nuts, and the usual vegetables I bought each week, I began adding mushrooms.

Lots of mushrooms. Sometimes I filled two produce bags, and whenever the market had those fancy boxed mushrooms, I bought all of them. I wondered how long I could eat these mushroom-filled meals and go without meat for Magdalena's sake. I wondered how long she could go without it. More urgently, I wondered how long Ringo would go without my bribes before deciding it was time to rant and tattle at my window again.

Ringo must not have understood I had cut him off. He continued to bring me gifts, which I added to the basket that was now just about full. In truth, I didn't want to stop feeding him. Even though he was just a bird, his devotion and faithfulness made him feel like a friend. I wanted to continue the relationship, but there was only so much I could handle in those final days with Magdalena.

I was growing exhausted, and not only from my daily patrols of the neighborhood. The chop-chop-chopping of vegetables every night was far more tiring than just throwing meat in the oven. Staying out late to follow Magdalena to the inn and visiting Mario afterward also depleted me. The weather began growing colder, and I heard talk in line at the market of coming storms. I operated in a fog, drunk on fatigue. My body kept moving while my head stayed a few paces behind. I didn't think this could last.

38

At last the lice and all their tiny eggs were gone. We were done with the mayonnaise treatments, but Magdalena still came every night for dinner. In this way, I held on to her.

Cecilia continued to join us. She was eerily quiet. She was patient. I could feel the chill of her, that sense of someone standing behind me, but she did not draw attention to herself. She simply stayed with us, watching and waiting.

Lemons were no longer necessary. I would have preferred that Cecilia come only when we called for her, but what could I do? She'd grown comfortable in my house. I had no good reason to tell her to leave since she didn't bother us. In fact, she took it upon herself to be helpful.

I began finding tiny piles of dead silverfish on my kitchen counter. I found their corpses on my bedroom dresser, in the bathroom sink, and in corners on the floor. It was disturbing how many Cecilia killed. I was certain she'd exterminated every last one when I started finding dead spiders and roaches in little piles, but every now and then another dead silverfish would show up. Never would I have imagined so many had been hiding in my house.

One night, Magdalena sat at the table in a green terrycloth jumper that looked like a bathing suit cover-up. She was staring into her phone. I'd just swept up three roaches and a small wispy pile of daddy long-legs from the floor, and then tossed them out the back door. Returning inside, the girl's back was to me. I could see she was looking at a picture of someone. Quietly moving closer, resisting the urge to lean over her shoulder, I saw a man's face. His complexion was darker than Magdalena's, but their features were so similar I knew who it had to be.

"Do I look like him?" she asked without turning around.

"Is that your—" I didn't say the word.

"Looks like it."

"Where'd you find the picture?"

"He's one of my mom's friends on Facebook."

I nodded, wondering how I could ask if she was going to contact him.

"He has a wife," she said, as if anticipating my question. "And a little daughter. I don't want to—" She lowered the phone to her lap so I couldn't see it anymore.

At the sink, I faced the duct tape over the window and washed my hands with warm water. I'd never considered her father a risk. She'd never mentioned him. I thought her mother was her only way out of town.

"Does he know about you?" I asked.

She didn't answer right away. I turned off the water and closed my eyes, letting my wet hands drip into the sink.

"My mother never told him."

I turned around and wiped my hands on my pants. "Do you want him to know about you?"

To my relief, she shook her head.

I brought her a glass of milk made from soybeans. I'd found it at a Norwood grocery store and bought several cartons, since Dorado's Market didn't carry that kind of thing. Then I sat down in a chair across the table from her. For the first time, Magdalena looked genuinely lonely. She was almost always alone, but she usually seemed energized by something deep inside her own mind. Now, that was missing. I myself was depleted, and yet in that moment, I would have given anything I had left in me to help her get back to herself. Playing this make-believe motherhood was not all love and joy. The instincts that came with the role threatened my own self-preservation. But at that point, I couldn't stop playing.

Before she left for the inn a spell of energy seemed to return. She rapidly tapped at the phone. When she was done, she glanced up and our eyes met. She was surprised to see me watching—like she'd been caught at something.

"You decided to contact him?"

"I didn't tell him who I was," she said defensively as she got up from the table.

"Then what was the purpose of your communication?"

She adjusted her green terrycloth jumper, pushing down the waistband. "I just asked if he could tell Juliette that her friend Magdalena is trying to get ahold of her." She looked back at me, and although she didn't quite smile, I could see the satisfaction in her eyes.

I understood. If her mother never told this man he had a child, she most likely didn't want him to know. By this cunning coercion, Magdalena might finally get her mother to reply. And I might finally lose her.

39

I've run out of paper again. I asked for more from one of the high school volunteers, an unfamiliar young man with long frizzy hair. I'd mistaken him for a girl until he told me his name was Dave. Dave said there is no paper to spare. They'd given me all they had. One of the Sisters is going to Norwood for supplies in a few days, and he said he would ask her to buy some. But these thoughts and memories won't wait. I've taken to writing notes and key words on tissue from the box beside my bed—something small I can hide and later throw away once I've transcribed it. The tissue holds my thoughts for the day, but I don't want to use it all up. And I can't hold in my story any longer. I need to write it down so badly, I almost took to writing on the walls. I'm not just telling a story—I'm birthing it. It's going to come out whether I have paper or not.

I lie on my bed, reciting lines over and over in my mind so I won't forget what I want to say. But my brain can only hold so much. The thoughts are beginning to overflow.

My recitations are becoming fragmented. I can't seem to pull my head together, so I search the room for something else to write on. I kick off the comforter, and then I see it. The blank white bed sheet is equivalent to at least twenty or thirty pieces of paper. Pulling it out from its tuck under the mattress, I hold it close and affectionately rub my cheek against the scratchy cotton that faintly smells of bleach. Miracles are all around. It's just a matter of recognizing them.

Kneeling on the floor, I lean over the bed and begin to fill the white sheet with sentence after sentence. My pen doesn't glide as smoothly on fabric as it does on paper, and some of the words bend with the flimsiness of the material, but the story continues to flow.

Rapidly, the white space fills. I push the top of the bed sheet away and move to the lower half. The written section bunches up near my pillow and single words rise to the top of the folds—*crow, Mass, slice, blood, affair*—the building blocks of my story. Even alone, the words hold power. I find myself playing with the sheet, so that new words rise up—*sinful, ladder, secret, girl.*

There's a knock on my door. Frantically I gather the sheet and ball it up in my arms. Without understanding my predicament, to anyone else the writing might appear destructive, possibly even crazy. I stuff it under my comforter and set pillows on top so it's buried deep. Staring at this lump on my bed, only slightly larger than the lump of guilt in my throat, I call out, "Who is it?"

There is no answer. The door simply opens.

"They tell me you haven't left your room since the night I had dinner with you." Sister Rosario approaches me. "And you barely eat what they bring you."

I close my eyes. "I am fine, Sister. I really am."

"This is temporary," she says, sitting at the edge of my bed. "Things are settling. You will have a normal life again."

I nod. I trust her.

"I've talked with Father Candido about finding a place for you to live. There is a house in Norwood—" She keeps her eye on me to gauge my reaction.

I nod again, although I have no interest whatsoever in moving there. Sam's Town is my home. I'm not sure why I want to stay, seeing how I've been treated, but I know I belong here.

"It can be depressing for a young woman like you to stay in a place like this. I want to get you back on your feet again."

"Thank you, Sister. But I assure you I am not depressed. I appreciate the time here to reflect." She eyes me, searching for truth in my words. "In fact, I have been writing down what happened to me, making sense of it in my mind."

"Writing is a good exercise for the spirit."

"Yes, it's helpful. But I've run out of paper. I asked Dave, the volunteer boy, to bring me some, but he said there is no more. I really need some."

"Paper?" she asks. I nod. "That's all you need?" I nod again. "And that will make you happy?"

"Yes." I smile.

"Very well," she says, standing up and smoothing down her navy-blue dress. "I have a notebook I can give you."

When she gets to the door, I say, "Sister?"

"Yes?" She turns back to me.

I can't get too sentimental with her. She's not that way. She would be uncomfortable if I told her how much I appreciated all her kindness. Instead, I keep it simple. "Thank you," I say. "For always helping me."

She nods and a rare smile comes through. "It's my job to bring God's light to the people." She stands with her shoulders high as she says, "I cannot shine if you don't shine."

She leaves, and I sit with those words. It's her job to bring God's light to the people. All the people. Even someone like me. That's why she does what she does. The simplicity of her purpose is breathtaking. She wants me to shine.

Soon, she is back with a notebook and a plate of food—like a bargain. I do my part and eat every last bite. Leaving the empty plate on the nightstand, I spread out the bed sheet and transcribe the words onto those magnificently blank pages. Then I move on to the rest of my story. I feel Sister Rosario's intention lighting me up inside, and it gives me the energy to stay up all night.

40

Magdalena walked through the back door as I pulled the casserole from the oven. She wasn't wearing her usual colorful clothing, but instead wore black spandex pants and a black sweatshirt. She didn't speak to me or look at me. A strange melancholy appeared to be upon her that night. Her phone stayed on the kitchen counter while she tucked herself into that small space behind the loveseat and stared mindlessly up at the painting on the wall. I didn't know what to say or do. Had her father replied in some negative way? Or, like her mother, had he simply not replied at all?

In an effort to pull her out of her sadness, I'd added more mushrooms to our meal—raw sliced mushrooms on top of an already mushroom-packed casserole. At the table, she ate every last bite on her plate and even forced down seconds, as if this might cure her. But no amount of mushrooms seemed to help. After dinner, she went back to her private spot and stared at the wall.

I couldn't stand it anymore. I had to ask her what was wrong.

"I heard back from her," she told me.

"Oh?" Her mother. "What did she say?"

"She said she doesn't want me."

I brought my hand to my mouth and closed my eyes. Of course I didn't want her mother to want her. I wanted Magdalena to stay here with me. Still, I couldn't help but feel sorry for her being rejected like that.

"She says I'm far better off here with my grandmother. She wants me to leave her and my father alone."

"Maybe you are better off here," I said.

"I hate this place."

I was quiet. What could I possibly say?

"I don't belong here. She didn't belong here either. I thought she'd understand."

I stood above her, leaning on the loveseat, listening to the wind at my front window. I felt a cold presence and knew Cecilia was there too. But Magdalena wouldn't look at either of us. She just stared at the painting. The heater rumbled as it tried to cough out some warmth.

I had an idea. I went to the basket beside the door.

"Remember that crow?" I said, sitting on the floor beside her. "The one I told you about?" She nodded without looking at me. "He still brings me things," I said. "He left these in my planter." I held out gold-rimmed sunglasses with light turquoise lenses. She took them from me and examined them.

"They're cool," she said halfheartedly.

"It's hard to believe he managed to carry them. Such a clever bird," I said, hoping to entice her with Ringo's latest feat, but she only nodded. "You can have them," I told her.

She slid them over her eyes. They looked like the kind of thing she might wear in Hollywood even though she no longer had a reason to go. "Thanks," she said, leaning back against the loveseat and closing her eyes behind the turquoise lenses.

The following night, Magdalena showed up at my house again. The sunglasses were set on the top of her head, and she still wore the same black clothes. The girl was in mourning. She had lost a mom she never really had. I understood the feeling, having lost children I never really had. I tried to talk to her but she didn't seem to hear me. She returned to her spot behind the loveseat, her sadness lit up by the pale glow of her phone.

I had no idea how to help her through this. Too tired to try anything else, I set the dishes to soak, swept up a small pile of dead bugs on the floor, and sat down at the kitchen table. Resting my head on the Ouija board, I closed my eyes. The chill in the room kept me from falling deeply asleep, but I did drift off. My mind craved rest. Only when I heard the back door slam shut did I open my eyes. Magdalena had left for the inn. It was time for me to go.

Grabbing my coat and forcing my tired body to keep going, I headed out into the cold, windy night to follow the girl.

Raising a child was a mystery to me. Taking one on as a teenager was even more complicated, and then having a teenager with supernatural abilities took those complications to the extreme. Yet even this difficult, exhausting time felt like a blessing. I was convinced that through some kind of divine intervention, Magdalena had come to make me a mother. Having finally been initiated into that ancient role, no difficulty, inconvenience, or exhaustion could make me give up on this child. Even with all her complications, her darkness, her tainted history, her mysterious ways, and her growing melancholy, Magdalena was mine.

Hidden behind the bushes at the yellow house, I closed my eyes while I waited for her. I was hoping to catch a bit of rest before she came out from the inn, but I fell into a deep sleep. The heavy dreamless slumber captured me and held me hostage until three in the morning, when a slap on the face woke me.

"ake up!" It was a woman's voice. "Wake up! What are you doing here?"

Branches poked at my skin, reminding me where I was—in the bushes. Stumbling out from my hiding spot, I brushed off my coat and saw Gina, a checker at Dorado's Market. Her husband stood beside her, pointing a flashlight at my face. "I'm sorry, I'm so sorry," I said, squinting at the light and tightening my coat to protect myself from the forceful wind.

"What in the world were you doing in the bushes?" the husband asked.

"I don't know," I said, pushing my hair away from my face as the wind blew it about. Off in the distance, a frantic bell buoy warned of trouble.

"Did you know you screamed?" Gina asked with her hands on her hips. "Did you realize you screamed while, for some weird reason, you were sleeping in our bushes? And this," she pointed to the window, "is the baby's room. You woke him up."

"I'm sorry—I must have had a nightmare. I didn't know—"

"I got her." A familiar voice came from the street. "I'll take her home. She sleepwalks sometimes. Nothin' to worry about." It was Frankie California. "I was up getting a glass of water and saw her through the window. Knew she must be sleepwalking again so I followed her. Come on, Dottie, I'll get you home." This lie of his was about to save me, but it also unnerved me. Had he followed me and watched me this whole time?

Frankie took hold of my arm, like he had all those years ago down at the water, and led me away. I could hear Gina saying something to her husband—something about me being crazy. I closed my eyes until we were far enough away that the wind was louder than her words.

"Now I don't want you to get me wrong," Frankie whispered as we walked the dark, cold streets. "I'm a big believer in privacy and minding my own business, but here's the thing." He tightened his grip until it was slightly uncomfortable. "I got no interest in the people from my past, but some of them still got interest in me. You know what I mean?" He didn't give me a chance to answer. "With all this talk of a stranger in town, I gotta make sure he's not here for me. I gotta be careful. I gotta watch my neighbors closely. Make sure they're not betraying me." He stopped on the corner and turned to face me. With his hands grabbing my shoulders, he said, "When I see you leaving late at night, I gotta wonder what you're up to. Did this guy lure you into some kind of plan? Is he trying to get to you 'cause you live next door to me?"

"Oh, heavens no. No, no no," I said, trying to pull away from his grip. He held tight.

"Shh, shh, don't go waking any more neighbors." He led me into an alley. The wind battered the metal trashcans beside us, rattling the lids, and tree branches scraped against backyard fences. There in the dark, in the hands of an ex-mobster, I feared for my life.

"Why you out this late, hiding in those bushes?" he asked.

"The girl next door," I told him. "Magdalena." I swallowed at this admission, and my speech became unsteady. But I had to tell him everything in order to protect myself. "It was brought to my attention her grandmother drinks and neglects her. I've allowed the girl to come to my house so she can feel safe." My voice was unnaturally high, as if I were on the verge of tears. "I feel protective over her now, and when I noticed her leaving late at night, I followed her—to be sure she's okay. She's just a girl and I'm only making sure she's safe."

A trashcan lid crashed to the ground, startling me. Dogs barked and a porch light went on. Frankie grabbed my arm again and pulled me farther down the alley.

"Where does she go?" he asked.

"The inn."

"What she doing there? Those ladies got her into some nasty business?"

"Absolutely not!" The thought made me clutch my stomach as if I might lose my dinner. "She's not that kind of girl. She sees ghosts," I explained. The truth seemed rather tame compared to his suspicions. "They have her conjure ghosts for their guests, and it brings in business."

"So you go out at night to follow this girl? A girl who runs a ghost scam at the inn?"

"No, it's not a scam. It's real. I've seen her talk to ghosts."

"All right, all right," he said. "Let's say it is. All I wanna know—is there anyone else you talk to out here at night? Is there anyone talking to you about me?"

"No!"

He eyed me there in the dark, as if he knew how to spot a lie. His stare interrogated me for a good minute and I held my most truthful face. Finally he tugged my arm again and led me back home.

At my gate, he stopped and said, "I'm the kind of guy you want looking out for you, okay? I got your back as long as you got mine." I nodded and looked toward Magdalena's house. I hadn't seen her return home safely. There were no lights on. I had to believe she was asleep. "You let me know if you see anything. You understand?"

"Yes, I understand. I will," I said. "I promise." I was tempted to tell him about Benjamin—maybe it would ease his concern over the stranger having come for him—but I couldn't bring myself to do it.

He eyed me again for a moment. I wondered if he could tell I was keeping something from him. But then he said, "That girl—don't let her fool you."

I said nothing. I had no idea what he meant.

"Get some sleep, Dottie." And he let me go.

42

It was rare to see the Norwood police come out to the peninsula. I was at my window the morning they came. The rain had eased slightly after a heavy downpour. Two officers stood on the porch next door talking to Buttons while neighbors watched from the sidewalks under their umbrellas. I opened my window to listen as the police assured the old woman they would do everything they could to help her find her granddaughter. That was how I learned Magdalena went missing.

The last time I saw her was at the inn, the night Frankie escorted me home. For two days, there'd been no sign of her. I assumed she had locked herself in her room, mourning her mother's rejection. I had no reason to believe she was gone.

After the police came, I told myself not to panic. There had to be a logical explanation. I put on my raincoat and sat in the plastic chair in my backyard, watching through the knothole for Magdalena to come home. I was chilled and shivering. The winds whipped through my wet hair as I steadied my eye to the hole. The frenzied bell buoy never let up. Its sounds haunted me, reminding me of my mother's stories about the young ghosts stuck in the cove. With Magdalena missing, the old story took hold of my imagination.

When it got too cold outside, I sat in my red chair looking out the front window. I watched the wind blow leaves and even whole branches off the trees, and when Charmaine arrived, I watched the crows battle the storm as they faithfully followed her route. Ringo was back among them now, no longer captive to me. I'd chosen Magdalena over the bird, and he screamed at me for my betrayal. He flew up to the top of my tree and down to its bulging roots, then at my window like he'd done before, but the wind must have altered his flight and he slammed

against the glass. I screamed at him to stop. I wanted to close
the curtains but what if Magdalena showed up and I wasn't
there to see?

For days I alternated between the knothole and the front
window and ignored the housework. I didn't sweep, dust, or
make my bed. I left the dead roaches and spiders and silverfish
in piles on the floor. I barely ate the beans and rice I continued
to cook in case Magdalena came back. Dirty dishes stacked up
in the sink. I let everything go.

Lying in bed at night, I stayed awake well into the ghost
hours as my mind wrestled with possibilities. Had Magdalena
gone to Hollywood despite her mother's rejection? Did she go
there to meet the woman who didn't want her, to convince her
she was worth wanting? Or had her father discovered who she
was and taken her in, unable to ignore his beautiful daughter?
Could it be that she ran away to escape this town she hated? Or
had someone lured her away?

That was the thought nagging at me. If she was with her
mother or father, it would break my heart, but at least she would
be safe. Even if she had run off, she might not be in danger.
The clever girl could take care of herself. I worried she'd been
kidnapped. More cardboard signs had been hung on the trees,
and now Magdalena was gone. My gut told me Benjamin was
somehow involved. My guilt told me her disappearance was my
fault. Still, there was nothing I could do.

"Landslide" was playing through the speakers when I walked
into Dorado's Market. I bowed my head, made a quick sign
of the cross over my wet raincoat, and wandered the aisles,
shopping for food. The mound of ground beef behind
the butcher's glass case tempted me. The image of a small
hamburger patty, fried up with a little garlic powder, salt, and
pepper made my mouth water. I stood at the glass case, staring
at all that meat—steaks, chicken legs, pork chops—

"Can I get you something?" the butcher asked.

"No."

I must have spoken too sharply. He put his hands up as if

in surrender and walked away. "I can't," I whispered to myself. "She could come home any time."

Nuts, lentils, rice, beans. All these things were in my basket when I noticed someone had changed the album on the turntable. Joni Mitchell's "River" played overhead. The hint of "Jingle Bells" at the beginning of the song reminded me of the coming Christmas season. Would Magdalena be home by then? Would I have the opportunity to wrap presents for her? Would I have a companion to help me decorate a tree?

In the produce section, I gathered onions and garlic and set them in my basket. I was sorting through mushrooms when I became fixated on the song's lyrics, anticipating the next line. I'd heard it so many times before, but this time I froze when it came. I felt the skin between my eyebrows squeeze up, deepening my pronounced frown lines. Never had the voices in Dorado's Market spoken so intimately about my predicament as Joni Mitchell did that day.

When she sang about losing the best baby she ever had, the line struck me like a fist. I lost my balance and fell forward toward the mushrooms. They came tumbling out of the bin onto the floor, and I stumbled about trying to avoid them, smashing them beneath my feet.

Clarity sometimes shows up in unusual places. While on my hands and knees, cleaning up broken mushrooms, I came to a realization. A mother does not wait around for the police to find her child. She does not hide behind her guilt and fears, hoping someone else will do the hard work. A mother takes matters into her own hands. If I'd lost the best baby that I ever had, I needed to go and find her myself.

On the floor of Dorado's Market, surrounded by smashed mushrooms, I closed my eyes. I could hear the boy who worked there saying, "Ma'am, ma'am, if you move I can sweep this up." I could also hear other voices whispering things like "Odd Dottie," and "What a mess." But none of that mattered now. I knew how I could find Magdalena. Of course! The answer had been in my house all along, waiting for me.

43

Lemons were no longer necessary. She came every night whether I cut them or not. Nevertheless, I sliced several and set them beside the Ouija board. I sat at the table, placing my fingers on the planchette. The coolness of the kitchen and the thick energy I felt assured me she was there.

Cecilia would help me find Magdalena.

My hands shook in anticipation. They shook from the cold. I tried to steady them so the ghost could do her work, but I was too agitated, too chilled.

I pulled my hands away and blew warm air onto them, but the cold had penetrated down to the bones.

"I'm sorry," I said, looking upward. "I'm sorry. Hold on a minute."

At the sink, I ran warm water over my shivering hands. I stared straight ahead at the covered window. What had this child done to me?

"Okay," I said, sitting back down at the table. "Let's try this again." I cleared my throat and set my shaking fingers back on the planchette. Before I could ask a question, my hands were swiftly guided to the letter F. I swear, not a muscle in my body had pushed the planchette. What I once thought of as a sinful child's game now became somewhat miraculous. It had the power to unlock the mystery of Magdalena's disappearance.

My fingertips stayed light yet firm as Cecilia continued to the A, then T, then H, then E, then R. I had to pull my hands away. "Her father," I whispered. "Her father?" My eyes watered and I shook my head. "But if she's with her father." I looked across the table, as if at Cecilia. "Then there's nothing I can do."

All the turmoil came to an abrupt end. I should have been relieved the girl was okay. I should have been comforted knowing Benjamin had not hurt her, but it wasn't about Magdalena anymore. It was about me. Just like my other children, I'd lost her.

The table shook, and the planchette slid to the floor. The lights flickered and a chair fell over. And then another chair. Dishes tumbled from the counter, along with my coffee pot and toaster. It was clear Cecilia was as distraught as I was. She had been with Magdalena far longer than I had, and so I let her have this emotional release without trying to stop her. The ghost with the broken heart wreaked havoc on my kitchen and I left her to her destructive mourning. In the living room I found comfort on the couch, staring at the painting on the wall.

I'm convinced Magdalena saved my life that night. Had I not been so saddened about her leaving me for good, I would not have fallen asleep on the couch, where I'd been staring at the painted girl in the red dress. I would have gone to bed. If I had been in my bedroom when the disaster struck, who knows if I would have survived.

44

A faceless man wearing red, who I understood to be Magdalena's father, pounded on my front door, wanting in. I stood at the window, begging him to go away, but he had come for his daughter. I'd hidden Magdalena in the baby's room. She was tiny, just an infant, bundled up in her crib. I kept begging him to leave us alone, but the pounding intensified until he knocked the door off its hinges and it crashed to the floor. I woke up with a gasp. The crashing sound was so real, I was convinced the man was in my house. I needed to save the baby. Disoriented, I jumped up from the couch, and though my front door was closed and secured on its hinges, I headed toward the baby's room. But first I peeked out the window.

In the eerie glow of a full moon I saw something as terrible as my dream. The eucalyptus tree out front was no longer standing. It had fallen onto my house. In a panic, I rushed to the bedrooms to determine how bad the damage was. It was horrible. The trunk had smashed clear through the baby's room. The tree missed my room but the impact had launched the vanity mirror. Glass shards scattered all over my floor and bed.

The tree's shallow roots couldn't hold through heavy rain and aggressive wind. I would later learn the strong winds broke branches from several other trees in town, but mine was the only one that had completely fallen. I closed my eyes in understanding: this was the tragedy the crow foretold.

I ran out the back door and found the crown of the tree in Frankie's backyard. Peering through the branches over the broken fence, I called, "Frankie! Frankie!" He didn't reply. I went to his back door and knocked and knocked, but he didn't answer. There was only one other person I could turn to. I ran barefoot through the wet town all the way to the convent.

Sister Rosario dressed quickly and walked me back to my house, asking questions. I gave her answers, but I can't remember a single word said.

As Sister Rosario and I approached my back door, it suddenly opened from the inside. Mr. Henderson, my neighbor across the street, stood in the doorway.

"We've got a problem here," he said to Sister Rosario.

"How bad is the damage?" she asked.

"I don't mean the tree," he said, now looking at me.

He led us to the living room where Mrs. Henderson stood by the couch, wearing a robe under her rain jacket. Georjean was there too, along with several other neighbors all bundled in blankets and coats. They glared at me as I walked into the cold living room. At least seven people were right there in my personal space. The itching started up.

"So you're the one who took these," Georjean said, holding up the keys Ringo had brought me. O-l-s-e-n. That was what the gold letters spelled out—Georjean's last name. "What were you going to steal from me?"

I turned to explain about the crow, but she wasn't looking at me anymore. She was looking at all the items spread out on the living room floor. That was where they displayed Ringo's gifts, which they'd found in the basket beside the door. Every one of them belonged to the people of Sam's Town. And they weren't the mere trinkets I'd thought they were. I learned that the glass earring was not glass—it was Mrs. Henderson's diamond earring. The Saint Christopher prayer card in the plastic holder, I was told, had a credit card behind it. It was taken from William Brown's car, the same car where Ringo had found the garage door opener. One of the other keys Ringo brought to me started a boat and another opened my neighbor's backdoor. And the small tin box, with the owls on it, did not belong to a child. It was a pillbox that held Chuck Quinn's heart medication.

They discovered the Ouija board in my kitchen, along with broken glass and overturned chairs. They found Magdalena's rosary under the loveseat, her school notebook on the coffee table. Long strands of her hair were still in the bathroom trash and they found them because these neighbors of mine now felt entitled to search every corner of my house. They noticed the spots of blood on the linoleum floor, the cupboard and the wall. They commented on the dead roaches and spiders and silverfish that lay in small piles. It all looked so bad. It seemed as if it couldn't get any worse, but it did.

"She's been walking the neighborhoods, stalking the children."

"Gina found her hiding in the bushes under the baby's window at three in the morning."

"But how did she sneak into our houses to take all of these things?"

"It was not a man after all," Georjean said, and everyone understood what that meant.

The ominous tale of a strange man in town, advertised on cardboard signs, had been set off by one small fact—stolen items. Explaining this minor mystery had stirred the imagination of Sam's Town and fed the dark excitement we all craved. Now that the items had been found in my house, the story grew darker and uglier and was certainly more provocative than the truth. They would never believe me if I tried to tell them what really happened. Their story was too good to give up. I was the predator of Sam's Town.

"What did you do with Magdalena?" Georjean demanded.

If they'd known how much I loved the girl—if they'd known all I did to protect her, they might understand how preposterous it was to believe I would do her any harm. I winced at the accusation, but I couldn't gather enough breath to speak. "We know she was here. And now she's gone. What did you do to her?"

"Dottie," Sister Rosario said, taking hold of my arm. "Just take a deep breath and explain yourself." I could tell she wanted to protect me, but it must have looked grim, even to her. My itching grew unbearable. Sister Rosario mumbled something about getting Father Candido and rushed off, leaving me alone with these people.

It grew uncomfortably quiet. Men continued searching my house and the women stayed in the living room, waiting for me to say something. The struggling wall heater rumbled and spit out heat, but lost the battle against my split roof. Standing there shivering, I knew I had to somehow explain myself. *She's with her father. She's with her father,* I said in my mind over and over, but the words would not come.

Breaking the silence, Mrs. Henderson finally said, "Someone needs to call the police."

"Don't call the police again." Buttons was by the front door. I hadn't seen her come in. "Don't bring them into my business anymore," she said. "That child will come back when she's ready to come back."

Everyone quieted.

"You know where she is?" someone asked.

Buttons looked directly at me, as if we were in on something together. "No," she said. "But Dottie didn't do anything to her. Magdalena ran away."

Buttons must have known she was with her father. For some reason, she didn't want to tell the neighbors. I was willing to keep her secret as long as she confirmed my innocence.

The woman who hid her drinking at night in the privacy of her bedroom now stumbled across the living room to stand next to me. I could smell the wine on her breath. She leaned against the wall to steady herself and everyone watched as she strained her neck to look up at the painting of the girl in the red dress.

"My God. That's been here all these years?" she asked.

There was affection in her eyes and at last I understood why Magdalena had been drawn to it. Buttons reached up to touch the painting of her daughter, the one Mario bought at a yard sale next door all those years ago, and she lost her balance.

Gripping the frame for support, it fell from the wall. The old woman fell too. Three of the neighbors had to help her up and carry her to a kitchen chair while the others discussed what I'd been blind to all this time—the real reason Magdalena kept coming to my house. I thought back to that first day she came to my door with lemons and kept trying to peek inside. How did she know?

The painting of young Juliette Bravo was the final straw. Here was the neighbors' proof that I'd lured in Magdalena with a picture of her mother. The drunk woman's confirmation of my innocence meant nothing to them anymore. They held to their belief that I was responsible for Magdalena's disappearance.

I had to sit down. Cecilia was beside me. Though the cold masked her usual chill, I could feel the familiar sense of her, the way I'd come to recognize her presence. My voice had no power to make these people go away. Only Cecilia could help me.

I stopped scratching my neck and pointed at the things on the floor. My hand shook, but the ghost understood. Cecilia lifted the plastic coin purse and bits of sea glass into the air. No one noticed. I pointed again and the jacks left the floor. The plastic cardholder followed and then the periwinkle crayon and the pillbox, the garage door opener and eventually all the crow's gifts slowly rose from the floor. Everyone quieted. The objects circled in the center of my living room, creating a whirlwind. My neighbors backed toward the walls, spellbound, their mouths open in amazement. It would have even impressed Magdalena, if she'd only been there to see it. Small toys, jewelry, bottle caps—everything joined the gentle tornado of stolen objects. It was beautiful the way Cecilia commanded every item and kept them circling.

I still thought it beautiful as Cecilia tore each object away from the whirlwind and sent it flying toward my neighbors. The bike reflector, the fishing hook, the earring, the keys, the brush, the lighter, the glove. My neighbors screamed and ran for the door. I knew it would cause me trouble later, but at the moment, it felt like one of the nicest things anyone had ever done for me.

I didn't witness what the old priest did to successfully send my friend Cecilia to the other side. When Father Candido showed up that night, Sister Rosario said we had to go. All I could hear was his chanting as the old nun led me down the sidewalk away from my house. Later, in the rest home, was when I learned that the town's last landslide ghost was gone.

During that late-night walk I finally found my voice. I told Sister Rosario everything—the truth about the crow and my meatloaf bribes, and the way he began to bring me gifts. I admitted Magdalena came to my house every night and how I let myself believe she was my daughter. I told her the truth about Benjamin, how we'd met at the library, and how I thought he was dead—how Magdalena came to bring his ghost back, though I later learned it was Cecilia. I explained how I'd circled the neighborhood to protect the children and why I felt the need to follow Magdalena to Samantha's Inn every night. I gave this confession walking down the cold, wet streets of Sam's Town, and Sister Rosario listened. She didn't condemn me or tell me she believed me. She simply took me to Mario's room, set up a bed for me, and promised we would find a way to get through this too.

45

The doctor blamed it on the cold, wet nights I stayed out waiting for Magdalena, my lack of sleep, and my inadequate nutrition. I had neglected my body and made it vulnerable. He diagnosed my high fever, body aches, and vomiting as a winter flu. It certainly could have been a virus, but I knew it was more than that.

Each time I had lost a child, severe sickness took me to the doors of death, as if my mothering instinct pushed me to follow the departed little soul. Magdalena hadn't died, but my body was reacting as if she had.

I knew I wouldn't find the living girl on the other side, but I was tempted to take my chances on finding her *from* the other side. I'd never locate where her father lived while trapped in this body of mine. But there was a chance I could find her if I was dead. And she would see me! Magdalena, the sensitive, could interact with my spirit, and I could follow her throughout her life the way Cecilia had. There'd be no walls, no barriers blocking me from the girl. It wasn't suicidal, this solution I came up with. It was more like giving in—allowing my sick body to take me to that final destination I'd been taught to look forward to my whole life. What better heaven than days and months and years of uninterrupted Magdalena.

My temptation to be with her spiked my fever and nearly drained the life out of me, but the survival instinct is not an easy thing to overcome. Deep inside, without regard for my resignation, healing took place. My mother was right about the miraculous nature of bodies. I woke up in Mario's room on the fifth day, fever free. My hope for a natural death was lost.

Though I was no longer sick, I wanted to stay in bed. I wanted to sleep, and dream about her. I obediently took the pills Sister Rosario gave me, spending my time staring at ceiling tiles, the walls, or sometimes at Mario's sleeping body. The residents from the hall peeked in on me and treated me like a curiosity, but the medicine kept me from growing too nervous.

I would find my rhythm again—slow and dull, yet safe. I would get back to the old me who could accept a lonely life in the rest home. I knew I'd always be haunted by this short, miraculous time with Magdalena, but it was just a blip. This reality, sharing a sterile room with my lifeless husband, felt more like the life I'd been born to endure. I believed what the years said about me more than I believed those errant months.

And yet I couldn't deny that my short time with Magdalena had changed me. I had to resist an energy that came now and then, whispering for me to get out of bed, telling me to risk the adventure of being fully alive. I shook my head at the suggestion each time I heard it. This was how I was meant to live the rest of my life: beside Mario, under the protection of the Sisters. I believed that was the only way to repent for all the things that I had done.

Until the day the crows came.

46

I heard the crows outside my window. At first I thought they were just passing by on Charmaine's route, but their cawing persisted. They seemed to be circling the rest home. I listened. I waited. And then she came.

The lady I'd watched through my front window, the one who took a moment every day to check if she had a letter for me, the one who was despised by the community for keeping company with the crows—this was the lady who walked into my room. It was the first time I'd seen her up close, really up close. Lethargic from being bedbound, I thought my senses were playing tricks on me. But it was no trick. She was really there. And in the confines of this lifeless little rest home, the bizarre story that was now my life was about to get stranger.

Charmaine stood before me with an envelope in her hand. She set it on the nightstand beside my pills.

Just as I'd been intrigued to finally see her up close, it seemed she found her own fascination with me. She was gentle the way she eyed me, almost childish in her curiosity. I was the woman behind the window. She was the woman behind the mask. Face to face, we took the opportunity to really look at each other. I noticed she had large freckles around her deep-set eyes. Her thin eyebrows were trimmed into sharp arches. The grays in her salt-and-pepper hair made wispy escapes from the braid, and her ears protruded forward—a likely consequence of wearing that mask all those years. She smelled like Bengay, and the breathing sounds she made against the mask were like petite gusts of wind.

When our quiet exchange was no longer satisfying to her, she cleared her throat and spoke. "It is a good bird, the crow. He not here for trouble. He here for good. A messenger." Her English was choppy, her accent unfamiliar.

"Well," I said. "If only I'd understood his message." She nodded. "But what could I have done? The tree was going to fall no matter what."

"Too loose in the ground," she said.

That was a curious way to put it, but I agreed with her. "It was." We both nodded. It felt good to talk about it. "How do you think he knew?"

She pointed upward. "God tell him."

It was a sweet notion, but she sounded like a child. I began to wonder if she thought my admission into this rest home meant I could no longer comprehend complex ideas.

"It can't be that simple," I said, not meaning to sound condescending, but there was a tree on my house, for goodness' sake. "Why wouldn't God just tell me? Why give that kind of message to a bird?"

"We not listen," she said. "The bird listen."

Again, her answer was too simple to take seriously but I appreciated her staying to talk with me. We were connecting, Charmaine and me. I could feel it.

"When you not talk, you learn to listen in powerful way," she said. I believed she spoke from experience. I had never witnessed her have a conversation with anyone else in our community and I felt honored to be the exception. It reminded me of the times Magdalena had opened up to me. I couldn't help but wonder if an outcast could only truly be heard by another outcast.

"Can you—" I motioned with my hand to remove her mask. "No."

"Why?" I asked. "There's no tree in here. Don't you wear it to protect yourself from the eucalyptus?"

"No," she said. "I wear to protect you. And all people in town."

"What on earth would you be protecting us from?" I asked, sitting up. "Would you show me? Please?"

She hesitated for quite some time. I waited as she seemed to consider my request. Finally, she lifted her chin high, brought her hand up to her face, and slowly pulled the surgical mask down. I was speechless. Her mangled nose and mouth were scars of some terrible brutality. Her lips were but coarse pink strips of skin forming a small opening that wouldn't completely close. But they managed a smile for me, a strange uneven widening that revealed both gums and teeth in such excess she looked like a growling dog. My face must have revealed my horror. Graciously Charmaine put the mask back on.

"I'm so sorry," I said. The poor woman had been hiding this awful truth all those years without a hint of self-pity. Had the people in town known her tragedy, might they have shown her more kindness? "I never would have known," I said. "You face the world with such confidence."

Her eyes told me she was smiling under her mask when she said, "I know who I am."

I was beginning to realize there might be something more to her simple words, something wise about the plainness with which she spoke, but our conversation came to an abrupt end. Two volunteers peeked into my room and caught her at my bedside. The young girls in their striped uniforms said Charmaine had to leave, no one was allowed in my room. I explained that she'd come to deliver mail, but they told her to leave it at the front for me next time, and they quickly escorted her away.

Charmaine was gone in a flash, but her last words remained. *I know who I am.*

They were a gift, those five words. They opened up my truth. It was not instantaneous. You might say the words initially just poked a hole into my truth. Really, it took all this time writing my story to reach a point where I could grasp their impact, but I can now say with certainty that Charmaine's words influenced what I chose to do once I read the letter.

When she left, I immediately reached for the envelope she'd delivered, wondering who in the world would write to me. Possibilities crossed my mind as I tore it open—my mother, my father, Benjamin, even Magdalena—but never in a thousand years would I have guessed who had really written to me.

Susan McIntosh. *The* Susan McIntosh from *Beyond the Veil Magazine.*

The typed letter explained she had heard about my ghost, the crow, the tree, and the missing girl. Sam's Town had been on her radar for years, but none of its stories had ever piqued her interest quite like mine. Would I be willing to tell her what really happened?

Despite the pills, and despite the defeated state I'd reached, something inside of me awakened. Susan McIntosh wanted to hear my story. Through her, the rest of the town would also hear it, and there was a chance I might finally be understood. I was not a predator or a monster, or any of those other terrible things the town had labeled me. *I know who I am.* I'd kept silent for so long, they couldn't know me. It was time I tell them.

And that was how I came back to life. My mind filled with thoughts and perceptions and memories and hopes that I might include in my letter to Susan. For the first time, I pressed the red button beside my bed to make a request. In fact, I made two requests. One was for a stack of paper and a pen—to begin my letter. The other was for some mushrooms—to end my sadness.

Once they brought me the paper and pen, I sat at the desk and tried to gather my thoughts, but I was distracted. It was cold. I pulled a blanket from the bed and wrapped it around me. The air conditioner was dreadfully high. They'd said it was to keep germs down, but I wondered if they were trying to weed out the weakest of us.

"Focus, Dottie, focus," I said, closing my eyes.

"What do you need to focus on?" someone asked.

Startled, I opened my eyes and tightened the blanket around me. I turned to find a white-haired lady in a wheelchair.

47

My letter is complete. I close my eyes and just breathe while I hold the thick stack of papers to my chest. It's only paper and yet it feels sacred. Somehow, I am in these pages. Magdalena is in them too. My fragmented life appears whole in writing, as if the retelling shapes it into something meaningful. I understand now that the library must be full of broken people who held their pieces together with words.

The regulars are lined up in their wheelchairs as I make my way down the hall, among them Henry, Buck, Gigi, Natalie. My head is down, but I can feel them watching me. I am carrying this stack of papers like it's my baby, protective and proud. Before I send it off to Susan, I must honor my word. I told the Centenarian I would share my story with her once it was all written down. Without changing from my robe and slippers, I take the now completed pages to her room.

The old woman looks virtually dead in her bed. It can't be much longer before she loses her last thread of life. I try to wake her, but I have a feeling she's already had her final waking moment. Her purple nightgown hangs over the foot of the bed and she is wearing a white hospital gown like Mario's. I pull a chair close beside her and sit down so I can read the entire letter to her. Her body gives no response, not even a twitching of the eyes, but I read every last word.

When I'm done, I wait a moment in the chair. I know she's too far gone to respond. The waiting is for me. I'm breathless, not so much from reading as from hearing aloud all the things that I'd done. I am not the same person I once was, and I'm uncertain how I go forward as the new me.

Back in my room, Mario is awake. He is uncharacteristically alert. His eyes are wide and they don't seem as empty as usual.

I'm pleased. I want to sit with him and spend some mindless time beside him talking about small things—the food they serve here, the trouble with the hot water in our shower, the hole I plan to mend in his robe now that I have more time. I want to forget the difficult things for a little bit and engage in trivial talk, but before I reach his bed, I stop in the center of the room. The sight before me doesn't register right away. I have to blink my eyes several times to believe what I see. There, on the edge of the desk, is a small pile of dead silverfish. I look around the room.

"Cecilia?"

I don't feel her presence. It doesn't seem like she is here right now, but I know without a doubt she was here. I wipe away my sudden tears and can't help but smile at her craftiness, fooling the old priest. My invisible friend did not leave Sam's Town after all. And I smile wider at her faithfulness, coming back to see me.

I press the red button on the wall once again.

"Yes, Dottie," I hear.

"I need a lemon." I can feel my voice quivering, not from anxiety, but from joy. "Please, could someone bring me a lemon?"

"Sorry. We don't have any lemons. I can put in a request for you."

"No need," I say, knowing I will not wait days for this request.

The church bell chimes twelve times. I change out of my robe and put on the clothes I wore when I first arrived a month ago. I am afraid Sister Rosario has warned everyone to stop me if I try to leave, so I keep my head down and even hold my breath as I head for the door. But the girl at the front desk does not pay attention to me. I don't think she recognizes me without my robe, or maybe it's that tiny phone of hers that has her hypnotized.

Outside it's cold but the sun has broken through the clouds.

I walk the streets holding my hand to my forehead to block the glare. I don't care who sees me. Soon enough everyone will read my story, and I can deal with their reactions then. But my immediate concern is getting to my backyard for a lemon.

Approaching Anchovy Avenue, I ready myself for the shock of seeing the tree on my house in the light of day. My heart quickens at the thought of witnessing the destruction in clear detail, but imagine my surprise when I approach the house and see there is no tree—just dirt where it once stood, and a dented roof over the baby's room, now covered up with plywood.

Inside my house, I am surprised again. Ringo's gifts are gone. The Ouija board is gone. Everything is cleaned up. It's as if all the things I remembered never happened.

I find the door to the baby's room boarded up. As I try to pry the board loose, I hear a voice behind me.

"Just leave it. Don't go in there. We got it cleaned up as best we could." It's Frankie. "You live alone. I didn't think you'd need that room anymore."

"Who did this?" I turn to him.

"I got some guys to come out," he says. "They're not professionals," he admits, squinting his eyes, "but they did it all for five hundred bucks."

"Why?" I ask. "Why did you do this?"

"I was away for one week and came home to reporters and TV crews," he complains. "They were all over your house and in my backyard. The last thing I needed was for them to get me on camera and let the wrong people know where I'm at. I headed right back out of town and called my guys to clean it up. They coulda made your roof look nicer, but they say it's saltwater plywood, so you're watertight and good for rain. They did a decent job on the exterior walls though. And they cleaned up my backyard, and your front yard and then repaired that damaged wall in your bedroom. I didn't see the point of wasting money on this other room you don't even need, so they just left the tree in there."

"It's still in there?"

"That portion of the trunk is big. It would've been expensive to remove. If *you* want to pay for the complete removal yourself, I can call 'em back." He pulls his cellular phone out from his pocket and lifts his eyebrows.

"You don't need to call them yet. I have to see if I can come up with the money."

He nods and puts the phone back in his pocket. "Just keep it bolted up and you'll never see it. You'll be fine."

"Thank you," I say, realizing I can leave the rest home now that my house is fixed. I can attempt to have my life back.

"I hear you're the predator." He smiles. "You wandering out at night and stealing little things from people's yards."

"I stole nothing," I tell him. "It was all a misunderstanding. There was a crow—he brought all those things to me."

He puts his hands up. "I got no problem with a little *pilfering*." He winks at me. "I done a little myself back in the day."

He has the wrong impression of me, but it's at least better than what the other neighbors think.

"They ever find the girl?" he asks.

I've disclosed her whereabouts in the letter. He will read it soon enough. "She's with her father," I say aloud for the first time. It sounds like such a simple ending to our story. Too simple. But sometimes, great stories do not have great endings. For the girl's sake I leave it at that, though I know myself well enough to foresee spending hours in the red paisley chair, staring out my window, conjuring better endings.

"I knew you had nothin' to do with it," he says. "I got instincts about these things. That girl struck me as the schemer. Not you."

I am not about to waste my time defending Magdalena, who had no other scheme than to make some money so she could find her parents. The ex-mobster seems to be doing a bit of his own story conjuring, and so I politely excuse myself to prepare for my final night at the rest home.

But first, a stop at the lemon tree.

48

It's dark and everyone is asleep. Mario is in his bed and I am at the desk. I only have a butter knife, but with enough pressure it cuts through the lemon's skin. Juice bleeds onto the desktop, and I wipe it away with the sleeve of my robe. Holding the lemon over a glass, I squeeze.

The lights don't flicker. Drawers don't open and close. There is no ghostly reaction. I wait, looking around for any kind of sign. After about five minutes, something strange does happen, though it's not what I expect. I smell broccoli. And the Centenarian appears. The woman who looked dead that morning while I read to her is up and out of bed. She can barely manage her wheelchair as she comes into my room, but she is wide awake and alert, wearing her purple nightgown again.

"Is she here?" she asks.

"Who? Is who here?"

"Magdalena."

I watch the old woman catch her breath as I try to understand why she's here. My mind doesn't know how to piece the information together to make sense of it. It's only a feeling when I guess, "Cecilia?"

She looks right at me, peering through those thick glasses, and nods. Chills cover my body. I wrap my arms around myself.

"But how—"

"Oh, it's far too complicated to understand." She raises her old arms and waves her hands, her fingers slightly curled. "Just accept it's me in here, borrowing the old body for a bit, and then we can finally talk about what really happened."

"But whose body are you borrowing? Who is this Centenarian?" I have to ask.

That's when she smiles. "Just as I waited for my husband, my mother waits for me."

"Your mother," I say. "This is your mother?"

She takes a deep breath. "She should've died years ago. This body is broken down, but she hangs on so I have a safe place to go." She reaches the old arms up around her shoulders—an embrace of sorts. A mother-daughter moment as bizarre as anything I've ever witnessed, even in a place like Sam's Town. "I tell her to move on. Go. Leave this world." She tries to laugh but the coughing starts up. I wait until she gets through the fit. "But she insists on waiting. That's the way mothers are."

I'm not afraid. I'm more confused than anything. There are so many questions I want to ask—like how can she, a ghost, get inside a living body? But I'm still speechless watching Cecilia speak through her mother.

"Every night, I made him a martini. He didn't like olives in it the way my father had." I can't figure out why she is suddenly telling me this story, yet I am captivated. I listen in awe, as if her words are little ghosts themselves. "My father liked his with a splash of olive brine and two olives dropped in. A dirty martini, my mother called it." She gives another phlemy laugh and places both old hands over her heart. "She thought it so racy to call it that—a *dirty* martini." She drops her smile and turns serious. "But my Cooper, he preferred a lemon—a little twist of lemon. Every night I cut one and peeled away the fruit so I could twist the rind in his drink. That smell made me anticipate him coming home." Now I begin to understand. "Magdalena had that tree. She was a smart girl. She didn't know why I was drawn to lemons, but she knew if she cut one open, I'd always come."

"Every time someone squeezes a lemon," I say, trying to make sense of what she's said, "you think it's Cooper. You're still waiting for him?"

"I was." She shakes her head. "But not anymore. Cooper died. When he passed through town, I could have followed him." She turns away to face the window. "It was about the time they hired Magdalena at the inn. She needed my help. The only way she could keep the job was if I played along with her performances. I couldn't leave her just when she started developing all that confidence. I had to let Cooper go on his own."

"And so you stayed. For Magdalena," I say.

"The poor child never had a mother."

"But she has her father now," I say.

"You didn't let me finish," she barks. Her nostalgic tone is gone, and she gathers the old body to wheel herself beside me at the desk. "I wasn't done spelling out the answer. Had you kept your hands on that Ouija board, I would have spelled out the second part—the most important part." She leans close and whispers, "Candido. Father Candido."

It makes no sense to me. "What does he have to do with any of this?"

"They caught her that night. As she left the inn. The priest and the child's grandmother were waiting outside. They took her away to fix her. Oh, they tried when she was little, but it never worked."

"Where is she right now?" I'm up from the chair.

"She's being held in that holy chamber of his, the Perch. I can't get through to her. They're guarding her with something stronger than sage. I've gotten through that old herb before, but this, this is something too potent."

"Why didn't you tell me immediately? When I first got here?" I grab my clothes from the drawer. "Why would you let her stay there all this time? It's been a month!"

"You didn't trust me when we first met. Remember? You said you wouldn't talk about Magdalena until you wrote the letter."

"But I eventually warmed up to you. You didn't have to wait this long."

"After all you'd been through, I realized you were not strong enough to go up against Father Candido. I still don't think you are. I figured if you got that letter out to the magazine lady, maybe she would come and help."

"There's no time for that. Magdalena can't stay there another minute. Tell me what to do and I'll do it."

"I don't have the answer. I can't get near her." She takes a deep breath into those rattling lungs. "This one is in your hands."

I make a quick visit to the bathroom to change into my clothes. I'm out in a minute.

"You're a fine storyteller," she says, still parked beside my desk. "The letter was magnificent. Better than the books you used to read to me. You know, I've really come to enjoy your company. If we lose Magdalena—"

"We're not going to lose Magdalena."

"Oh, we could lose her, all right. Don't fool yourself, Dottie." I look to her—the woman, the ghost, this strange combination of the two. "That child can't find peace here. Her spirit is too big for this small town. It's like putting a lioness in a backyard. She doesn't belong here."

I head to the door, not wanting to hear anymore. Magdalena is here, in Sam's Town. I'm not going to lose her again.

"You and I belong here," she says, and I stop. "But Magdalena? She's just passing through."

I turn back to her. "You don't really belong here," I tell her. "You know that."

"I've chosen to stay."

"But eventually you have to move on."

She shakes her head. "There's no telling where I'd go from here. I didn't lead the most virtuous life." She closes her eyes as if remembering, and then opens them again. "Father McKenzie refused to hear my confession. He would not forgive my infidelity. I died without a clean soul." With great effort, she raises her chin and straightens those hunched shoulders. "I'm staying in Sam's Town until they come drag me to Hell."

A coughing fit strikes again, and she bends over as her lungs beg for air. I'm certain it's the mother's reaction to her daughter's words. There is nothing I can do to help. I leave them to their moment and step out into the cold night to find Magdalena.

49

A hazy glow from the lampposts illuminate the church courtyard. It's almost midnight. The rain has stopped, though I can feel its imminent return. There is a faint light on in the Sisters' room. Father Candido's room is dark. Above the rectory, at the top of the metal stairs, is the Perch. The roof is covered with sleeping pigeons. All is still. Could Magdalena really be inside? I trusted Cecilia completely while we spoke, but facing the churchyard alone, my doubts grow.

The fountain doesn't run this late. There is no calming water sound to soothe my edginess. Instead I take comfort in the statue. A narrow light shines on Our Lady's face and praying hands, but the rest of her figure bleeds into the night.

Before taking the stairs, I kneel at the fountain and dip my hands in the cold water. Keeping them there, I let the cold enter my veins and recite a Hail Mary.

"—pray for us sinners now and at the hour of our death. Amen."

Still kneeling, I fold my shivering hands and gaze up at the holy mother. It's just stone, this Mary figure, but she is real to me. Growing up, boys were given superheroes, powerful men in capes. Mary in the long blue robe was a Catholic girl's superhero. Her power? She could love you to death. Tonight, that is my only weapon.

One step at a time, I quietly ascend the metal stairs. I don't have a plan. I don't even have proof the girl is here. All I have is a ghost's word.

Halfway up, my foot lands too heavily on a step and the noise wakes the pigeons. There must be a hundred of them now rising from the roof. Their collective flapping is loud enough to reach the Sisters' room below. I hear a door open.

"Dottie! In heaven's name, what are you doing?"

It's Sister Rosario. She bunches her long nightgown in her hands and holds it up as she hurriedly climbs the stairs behind me. Her nightgown is pink. I've never seen her in anything but her dark habits. She looks more grandmotherly than sisterly.

"She's here," I whisper. "Magdalena is here."

The door at the top of the stairs opens and a light turns on. It's Father Candido. He looks down on us.

"What are you two doing at this hour?" he asks.

"I'm sorry, Father," Sister Rosario says, taking hold of my hand. "She is confused. I'll get her back to her room right away."

The itching comes on suddenly. What have I gotten myself into?

"But why did you come?" Father Candido asks suspiciously.

"Father, she's just confused." Sister Rosario tries to protect me, but I speak up.

"Magdalena," I say. "I've come for Magdalena. I know she's here."

"Dottie, stop," the old nun whispers. "I can't keep protecting you. You have to pull yourself together," she pleads.

"Who told you?" he asks. "Who told you she's here?" His voice grows louder, like it does when his sermon is about to get scary.

"Father?" Sister Rosario lets go of my hand.

"Tell me how this information came to you," he demands of me. "Are you also talking to the dead?"

"Father." The old nun's voice is stern as she climbs the stairs. "*Is* Magdalena here?"

"I had to do something," he tells her. "How could I let the possessed child go on with that kind of life?" This question is his admission.

"No," Sister Rosario whispers in horror.

"She is here with the consent of her grandmother," he explains.

"Has *the child* consented to being here?"

"She is accepting the treatment," he says. "What kind of future can she have with demons guiding her and ghosts whispering in her ear? Her grandmother comes to see her every day. I pray over her every night. There is nothing amiss."

He believes what he says. It's clear he thinks he is doing the right thing.

"This," Sister Rosario hisses, "is not condoned by the church. They told you to stop this kind of thing." She pushes the door open and I rush up to follow her inside. The priest lets her by but stops me.

"How did you know?" His grip on my arm is tight. I don't answer. "Have they taken possession of your soul as well?"

He still has some kind of power over me. I bow my head. "No, Father," I say.

Sister Rosario comes out with the girl on her arm. Magdalena. It's really her. Her dark hair is uncombed and wild-looking, and she is squinting as if she's just woken up. A long black robe, like those the nuns wear, hangs on her, and her feet are bare.

"Take her," Sister Rosario says, pushing her out the door to me. "Get her away from him."

"Wait," I say. "She needs shoes."

The old nun in the pink nightie reaches down and grabs a pair of black boots—men's boots. She hands them to the girl and slams the door shut. Magdalena lethargically slips them on as we listen to the holy woman and the holy man yell at each other.

I hold Magdalena's arm, and through the black robe it feels skeletal. Up close I see her face has lost its fullness, and though her eyes appear pleased to see me, they seem too tired, too hungry to focus. I hold tight as I guide her down the stairs.

"Are you okay?" I ask. It's a terribly weak question in the face of this immense crime, but it's all I have.

She nods.

"Did he hurt you?"

She shakes her head.

"Did he feed you?"

"I ate the rice and vegetables. I wouldn't eat the meat." Even

through the suffering, she held to her convictions. The strength
of her will inspires me.

"Did you ask for beans or lentils instead?"

She nods. "They said I wasn't in a position to be picky."

Magdalena leans on me as we leave the church courtyard
and make our way out to the street. I hold her up and bear her
weight as we travel the wet sidewalks of Sam's Town.

"Exactly what did he do to you?" I ask.

"He tried to fix me again," she says. "He tied me to a chair.
He held me by the throat and chanted, calling out threats to the
devil and pleas to the holy army of angels and saints."

"That monster," I whisper. Her boots fall heavy on the
pavement. My heart falls even heavier.

"He kept me locked up in that room, and my grandmother
let him. She's as much of a monster as he is."

"I'm sorry. I wish I'd known sooner. I would have come for
you."

We don't speak the rest of the way. There is only the sound
of her boots and the lightly tossing bell buoy awakening with
the wind.

We reach my house and go through the back door. The
kitchen light reveals just how thin the already slender girl has
become. It sickens me that the old priest would allow this to
happen. I find a can of nuts in the cupboard. It's all I have
that isn't rotten. Magdalena sits at the table and tosses handfuls
into her mouth, chewing fast. I double check the refrigerator,
and while the vegetables and fruit have all gone bad, I find an
unopened carton of soy milk. I pour her a glass and sit beside
her, watching her drink it down. A chill hits me and Magdalena
glances up. Cecilia has arrived. For the moment, it almost feels
like we are back to who we were.

"I'm not safe here," she says when she's done eating. She
leans toward me, her elbows on the table. There is fear in her
eyes, something I've never seen from her. "I can't stay. I need to
get away from this place."

"But if we just expose what Father Candido did to you—"

"They trust him more than they trust anything I can say. They'll believe he was trying to free me from my demons."

"Where will you go?" I have to look away when I ask this.

"Hollywood. Back to my mother."

"I thought she said—"

"Come with me," she pleads. "You're the only one who could tell her what really happened. We can take the bus tomorrow. You don't have to stay long. Just long enough to explain why I can't live here anymore. Will you do that for me? Please?"

My stomach tightens. I want to bolt up every door in my house and keep her here with me, safe from the outside world. I want to hold onto her and never let her go. But looking at the girl with the wild uncombed hair and the ferocity in her eyes, I remember what Cecilia said. She is a lioness. And Sam's Town in not just a backyard, it's a cage.

"Please?" she says again, and this time she drops her head to the table, too weak to keep it up.

50

The bus stop bench is hard and the wind is freezing. Magdalena would not risk missing the bus, and so we stayed here all night. It stopped raining around four, but everything is still wet. I held the umbrella over her while she slept, and that kept her from getting drenched, like I am. My hair is as saturated as my clothes, and my shoes are like small pools in which my feet swim. I'm shivering but I'm not cold. A fierce heat burns inside of me.

Last night I told the girl I would accompany her to Hollywood and tell her mother how horribly she has been treated. I told her I would confirm that Buttons is a drunk and that the old priest held the girl captive in the Perch for a month as he performed daily exorcisms on her, and almost let her starve. I will explain how the people here will not hold it against Father Candido, but will blame the child, who has been looked down upon since she first arrived, a bastard. Together we will convince Juliette Bravo that Magdalena is better off with her than with her grandmother. No matter how difficult it will be for me to lose the girl, I know it's the right thing to do.

When I agreed to her plan her eyes lit up and she began to laugh, not like something was funny, more like an overflow of happiness. The sad truth was I'd never heard the girl laugh before. What a beautiful, joyous sound it was. It made me realize Father Candido had not broken her, and Sam's Town had not yet crushed her spirit.

Once we got to the bus stop, she fell right to sleep with her head on my lap, secure in my promise to help her. But I have stayed awake the entire night, pretending for the last time that she is mine.

The fantasy is unraveling.

It's almost morning. The sun is about an hour from rising

when a figure approaches. The hazy streetlight above gives it the impression of a ghost. Depleted and vulnerable, I can do nothing to defend against it. Am I finally seeing the real Cecilia? Has she come to accompany the girl to Hollywood as well? Or is this some other Sam's Town ghost coming to say goodbye?

As the figure gets closer, I see it's wearing a raincoat and holding a travel bag.

"I'll take her from here. You can go home now." It's Buttons. She sits right beside me, her arm touching my arm. I can smell the alcohol on her breath. I am sure she can feel my shivering.

"She asked me to stay." My voice trembles with my body. "I can't leave her."

"I'm her grandmother, for God's sake. I raised this child. Who are you to her? The neighbor who let her play with your Ouija board? Jesus Christ." She drops the bag to the ground and leans back against the bench.

"He kept her captive for a month." My voice still shakes. "And you let him. The girl is traumatized. She was abused."

"If there was any abuse, it was self-abuse." Her eyes are closed. She looks tired. "The door was unlocked. She could have come home any time. And we gave her food. She just wouldn't eat it." She gives a laugh that comes out of her nose. "The child is an actress. Like her mother. She told me she was ready to be healed, ready to rid her soul of those demons. But she was manipulating me." She opens her eyes and looks at me. "Like she's manipulating you."

Under the flickering streetlight, Buttons looks old—too old to be telling false tales. Is it possible Magdalena allowed this? Could she have orchestrated it all in order to convince her mother she was unsafe here? Did the old priest and her grandmother play right into her plan? Did I?

"I gave everything I had to the child, but there's no changing her," she says. The wine has soured on her breath. "She wants to be with her mother? Okay. She can take her chances in that Hollywood cesspool, if that's what she wants. But she's not showing up at my daughter's door with some oddball neighbor. I'll take her myself."

I try shaking Magdalena awake. She should have a say in this. Buttons grabs my arm. "Don't wake her. Let her sleep. She's a real pill when she hasn't had a full night's sleep."

The streetlight grows exceptionally bright, then it dims. It does this again and again, and only then do I realize it has been flickering all night, but I've been too distracted to register it. Cecilia isn't looking to interact with us. She is simply letting me know she's here.

The three of us, Buttons, Cecilia, and I, stay with the sleeping child before her final departure from Sam's Town. It's a pitiful trio of mother figures. I'm aware for the first time how unlucky this child has been, even willing to starve herself to break free from us.

"They're too much alike, Magdalena and her mother," Buttons says. "It'll be hell for both of them, but what can I do?"

"Will she even take her?" I have to ask. "Will she agree to take her back?"

"I called her after Sister Rosario called me tonight, chastising me for this supposed abuse I allowed." She shakes her head. "That's when I figured out what Magdalena had done. I had to let my daughter know what was going on. I told her this child wanted to be with her mother and resorted to ruining my reputation in town in order to get her way. You know what that child of mine said? She said she wanted her mother too." Her voice almost cracks, and she stops for a moment. "Said she would take Magdalena back if I came with her. She wants to make peace. *Now* she wants to make things right? After making my life hell?"

"Maybe you made her life hell too." It's Magdalena speaking. Her head still rests on my lap. Her voice is quiet but rage doesn't need volume.

"What a load of crap," Buttons snaps. Her hand is on Magdalena's arm now. "I did everything I could to save my daughter from herself. Tried to save you too." She gives a laugh. "You don't think I know who's here right now flickering those lights? You don't think I'm able to see what you and your mother could see?" Magdalena sits up and stares open-mouthed at her grandmother. I am shocked too. "Oh, I could see them, all right. But I resisted. I learned to shut them out so my soul would not fall to Hell. The way yours will if you don't change your ways."

"What if this place is my hell?" Magdalena says.

Buttons throws her hands up. "Then let's get you out of here. In a couple hours, the bus will come to take you away. Lord knows I did what I could. Whatever happens to you now, my conscience is clean."

It's quiet. I feel the loathing between them.

"Dottie," Buttons says, "why don't you go home now."

"Let her stay," Magdalena says.

"She's not coming with us." Buttons folds her arms and leans back against the bench. "That was not in the plan your mother agreed to."

"Fine," Magdalena says. "But let her stay till morning." She lies back down on my lap and reaches for my hand. She holds tight, like a child not quite ready to let go. There is no *thank you* or *I'm sorry*. There is no *I'll miss you* or *I'll always remember you*. No one has taught her to say or feel these things. There is just her hand, holding onto mine, and through it, I take in everything.

"I want to stay," I tell Buttons.

"All right, then. Suit yourself," Buttons says, leaning on my shoulder as if making use of me while I'm here.

The girl falls back to sleep, and even Buttons drowses, but I stay awake, watching the light flickering above and feeling Magdalena's hand in mine, hanging on to the very last thread of whatever it is we have.

Two Years Later

The crows hover over the sidewalk when Charmaine comes by, now that the tree is gone. Ringo is among them, but I can't tell him apart from the others. I have to make a lot more meatloaf than I used to, just to be sure he gets something. They all swarm down as I toss the meat bits onto the sidewalk, and Charmaine always stops to wait for them. She's become a new person to me since I discovered what was under her mask. The more I talk to her, the more I understand courage. And I've come to believe courage can be contagious. Sometimes I break the meatloaf into small pieces, taking longer to feed the crows so I'll have more time with Charmaine—and more time to catch what she has.

When I am outside with Charmaine and the crows, all the neighbors go inside and watch from their windows. Now they are afraid of me and I like it better this way. They say I've finally gone completely mad. I say my madness serves me well. I'm still an outcast here in Sam's Town, but I've been elevated to a dignified one.

They published my story as a series in *Beyond the Veil,* and the reception was overwhelming. Years of loneliness and these thoughts I keep in my head have translated into the magazine's most popular stories. Sales around the country almost doubled by the time the entire Magdalena saga had finished. Now I have my own column. The townspeople certainly don't condone the way I openly write about our little corner of the world, but no one has the audacity to confront me. And the way *Beyond the Veil* sells out so quickly now at Dorado's Market, I know they secretly can't wait to read it. Sometimes I write the truth I find around town and color it with fantasy, and other times I write lies that I make into truths. It's strange how stories have a way of shaping reality. If you believe something strong enough, it can change you.

It's been two years since Magdalena left town. The Miller twins are gone, and a new family with four young daughters has moved into the big turquoise house that was once an inn. When the Millers lost the ghost girl, business plummeted. Having no reason to stay, the twins drove their pink Cadillac back to Alaska.

Cecilia, on the other hand, has every reason to stay. Father McKenzie's refusal to forgive her has left her poor soul too afraid to move on. I've tried talking her through it. I had our new priest come by to hear her confession, which is an unconventional request, but he's kind like that. Cecilia's still here, though. Even the Centenarian's death couldn't move her along. I have a feeling she's grown comfortable in my house—like a homemade heaven. While I feel responsible for helping her to eventually leave this place, I'm in no rush. I enjoy the company.

Buttons returned from her month-long trip to Hollywood the same bitter old woman she was before. She claims to have made peace with her daughter, but she can't seem to make peace with herself. Once a week, I stop by with a mushroom casserole or mushroom soup that the melancholy old woman desperately needs. She's terribly mean to me when she first opens the door—chastising me for feeding the crows, condemning me for buying one of Cecilia's Virgin garden statues I found at the Goodwill, or complaining about the shoddy appearance of my plywood roof. But if I tough it out and let her unleash all that anger on me, she eventually invites me in to eat with her. She clearly knows nothing about what I've written in *Beyond the Veil*, too devout to read such a magazine. Once she starts on the wine, she tells me stories from Hollywood and shows me pictures on her phone of a vibrant Magdalena. It's my only connection to the girl. When she broke free from Sam's Town, she had to leave me behind. I've accepted that, but I still long to hear how she's doing, even if it means I have to befriend a woman like Buttons.

Father Candido was quietly sent to a home for aging priests

and was replaced with the newly ordained Father Benjamin. Sister Rosario watches him like a hawk, but no one else in the community realizes who he is to me. For legal reasons, the magazine changed his identity in my story and he became a pharmaceutical salesman from Norwood who came to the rest home on business. I was nervous when Benjamin first returned, but Sister Rosario brought him to my house, practically dragging him by the collar, to apologize and to promise he would honor his vows. And he has. He's not the dangerous predator I made him out to be—just a regular old sinner, like me. Every now and then, when we are alone in the confessional and I admit my sins, his old sins resurface in his eyes. It reminds me of our days at the library, and the spark that once brought us together is rekindled. Without his hands all over me, he's less selfish and is able to really look at me again. There is confusion. There is temptation. I admit there is a slight thrill to our longing, but ultimately there is safety, as Sister Rosario always waits outside the door for me. Best of all, there is a story.

I find them everywhere now. They overflow in my head and calm my anxieties when the tiny white pills aren't enough. I find them in the hall at the rest home, where I now stop and listen to the old tales before they die away with the ones who lived them. I find them on Mario's bed when I look into his blank eyes and try to make sense of why he stays. I find them when Frankie comes over to check how the ceiling is holding up and stays for a cup of coffee. The stories show up in Buttons's living room when we have dinner, and at my front window, where my view of the neighborhood is clearer and brighter now that the tree is gone.

I find them when the new little girls in town, who live in the turquoise house that was once an inn, come by to watch me feed the crows. Unaware of my reputation, they ask me questions about the birds. I tell them the crows talk to God, and how once one tried to tell me what God said. The girls ask if the birds are angels. I marvel at their imagination and say yes, the black birds are in fact angels. Now they come by quite often to help me feed the crows. I give them bits of meatloaf they hold in their little hands and throw out toward the sidewalk, giggling as the black birds swoop in. Their tangled hair, their brightly colored clothes, their squeals of joy bring out the old maternal instinct in me, and I always take them inside to wash their greasy hands before they leave. I've found if I keep a pitcher of lemonade in the refrigerator, they will stay a while. I haven't yet met their parents, who seem to have a lax approach to parenting. The oldest of the girls carries one of those cellular phones, and their mother simply calls when it's time to go home. It's still hard for me to believe there are four of them—four little girls!—sitting at my kitchen table the way Magdalena used to.

When they discover I have a tree in my house, they beg me to open the door Frankie bolted shut. How could I refuse? They climb the dried, rotted trunk. They find bugs on the tree and sometimes get scratched up from the parched bark, and yet there is something beautiful about watching them play make-believe. They bring to life a whole world in the confines of this small room. The walls are broken. The tree is dead. The caved ceiling is covered with plywood, but these little dreamers know how to make this place whole again. They conjure princesses and witches and dragons and mermaids—anything they need to survive the colorless days of life.

Material riches can never compare to richness of mind. These little ones intuitively understand that, and I give them this tree, this room, this devastated space to develop their riches, so when they reach the tedium of adulthood, they just might hang on to a bit of the magic they once knew at Dottie's house.

Sometimes I still go out back, sit in the plastic chair beside the fence, and look through the knothole. I know she's not there anymore, but if I stare long enough through the small hole, into the past, I can see her. Magdalena, the girl who unknowingly mended this damaged heart of mine. She's like a vision, a ghost, or maybe just a mother's daydream. It's not real. It never was with Magdalena. But since I don't live a life overly concerned with what's real, when the old melancholy comes back to haunt me, I know how to find her. Even on the grayest of days or when the Sam's Town fog grows thick as milk, I can still see the girl. And she stays with me, easing away my loneliness, until I close my eyes and let her go.

ACKNOWLEDGMENTS

Christine Amoroso, Mike Miller, Annie Quinn and Cindy Berg, I am so grateful for our weekly writers group and all you gave to make this a better novel. The reading and discussing, the questions and critiques, the laughter and tears, the encouragement and friendship—writing is far less lonely because of you, my writer family. Christine and Mike, I must also acknowledge the immense help you gave outside of writers group, always willing to be my second pair of eyes. I appreciate you both.

Thank you to Jaynie Royal and the team at Regal House Publishing for your care and support in bringing *Magdalena* into the world.

Michelle Dotter, thank you for your early edits that gave me clarity through the rewrites. Gabrielle B. McLean, Joan McMahan, Teri Ryder, Pam Sheppard and Deborah Parker, each of you offered valuable feedback and insights that helped me along the way, and I am so grateful.

Deborah "Atianne" Wilson, thank you for your ghost guidance. Our many conversations gave me clarity... and the chills!

Cinnamon Sary, thank you for reading several drafts of the story and sharing your creative wisdom with your mom. Our deep dive discussions always helped me see the way forward.

Thank you to my mom, Arlene Katnich, and to my three sisters Michelle Katnich, Terri Sullivan, and Gina Potter, for reading every manuscript I've ever written and for always cheering me on. And thanks to my dad, "Mutt" Katnich. Your stories and knowledge of commercial fishing were so helpful in the creation of Sam's Town.

To my husband, Tony Sary, thank you for supporting all of my dreams, and for truly being my best dream.